DEADLY CIRCUS
A WITCH IN THE WOODS

JENNA ST. JAMES

Deadly Circus

Jenna St. James

Copyright © 2024 by Jenna St. James.

Published by Jenna St. James

All Rights Reserved. No part of this publication may be reproduced without the written permission of the author.

This is a work of fiction. Names and characters are either the product of the author's imagination or are used fictitiously, and any resemblance to actual persons, living or dead, business establishments, events, or locales is entirely coincidental.

❀ Created with Vellum

I

"I'm telling you, Shayla, it was scary and awesome all at the same time." My stepdaughter, Zoie, slapped her hands to her chest as we strolled across the grass-covered grounds where Monte's Magical Circus had started setting up yesterday morning. "I mean, I've learned a lot from working with you and Dad here on Enchanted Island, that's for sure, but it was my first case alone." She laughed and waved a hand in the air. "Well, not exactly alone. Harlow and Needles were by my side helping to solve the case as well, but you know what I mean, right?"

Harlow Grimmson was the youngest recruit ever to come out of PADA trained as both a detective and in forensics. She was wicked smart, and leaned to the Goth side with her all black clothing, purple lipstick, and deadpanned deliveries. The half vampire, half witch supernatural was a perfect partner for Zoie.

Harlow and Zoie not only worked as an investigative team for PADA in their Remote Locations Division, but they currently lived together in town in a cottage that once belonged to both my mom and my grandma, GiGi.

"I understand what you mean," I said. "And, yes, I still remember my first case with PADA, and I totally understand how you're feeling."

I'd worked for the Paranormal Apprehension and Detention Agency for many years as a detective before retiring and returning home to Enchanted Island to become the game warden. I was afraid I'd be bored and miss the excitement of the job, but the last three years had proved to be the toughest and most exciting years of my life. Not only had I gotten married in that time, but Zoie's dad, Alex Stone, was also the sheriff of Enchanted Island, so I was asked to assist him and Detective Grant Wolfe a lot.

Needles, my talking and flying porcupine partner, sprang from my shoulder, his wings glowing purple and green. *"And I couldn't have been prouder, Princess. Miss Zoie and Miss Harlow both proved themselves to be excellent investigators."*

Zoie waved her hand in the air. "I'm sure if there had been a local paranormal law enforcement agency or even a PADA station nearby, they could have handled the investigation, no problem."

"Don't sell yourself short, Zoie," I said. "You and Harlow both deserve to be leading the Remote Locations Division."

Sadly, with supernatural crime on the rise over the last ten years, more and more PADA agents were being stretched thin when it came to covering locations. In response to the taxing workload, PADA recently created a Remote Locations Division, which meant Zoie, Harlow, and Needles would be sent to places that either didn't have a police presence or a PADA station nearby. With Harlow having acquired both a forensics degree *and* her detective's shield, she'd been chosen at only twenty-two to lead the team. Zoie, at only eighteen, had just received her detective's shield as well.

"You're the youngest team ever assembled by PADA," I said proudly, "and by solving your first case, you two have proven why you both deserved to be working Remote Locations."

"Absolutely!" Needles exclaimed as he landed back on my shoulder.

Zoie grinned. "And the best part is during our down time, Harlow and I get to help you out." She pointed to an elderly witch currently enchanting bubbles so the scenes inside change when commanded. "Which means I couldn't be happier that the game warden has been hired on to make sure the grounds don't get torn up and pollution is kept to a minimum while the circus is in town."

I smiled. "I'm glad you're enjoying this, and it's important the land on Enchanted Island is always respected."

"It's important to Black Forest King as well," Needles said.

Black Forest King was my dad.

As a Genius Loci, he was *literally* the heart and soul of Black Forest. As the heartbeat of the island, he had certain abilities. Two important powers were the ability to change the island's coastline when needed, and the ability to communicate with flora and fauna.

That last ability transferred to me when I was born. I, too, could communicate with the plants and animals on Enchanted Island. Which was why being the game warden was so important to me. I wanted to make sure the island was happy and healthy at all times.

That's why I'd insisted that I be present and on-duty while Monte's Magical Circus was on the island. Not that the mayor or the island council cared. As long as I did my job, I could set whatever hours I wanted.

"Don't let me forget to buy some cotton candy before we leave tonight," I said. "I promised the fireflies some."

Needles scoffed, his wings glowing red and black. *"You spoil them too much, Princess. Who ever heard of lightning bugs eating cotton candy and Pop Rocks?"*

Zoie giggled. "They do get excited when you bring them all that sugar, Shayla."

"It's a good thing fireflies don't have teeth, or they'd have cavities!"

I laughed. "See, so it's fine. No need to worry about cavities."

Needles scoffed. *"It makes them zip around the forest like their lights are on fire!"*

Because he was right, I simply laughed.

"Look over there," Zoie said, pointing to The Big Top. "Looks like they finally got the tent up last night after we left. And how *cool* is that fabric?"

The Big Top's towering canopy stretched high into the sky, the red and white fabric shimmering like Needles' wings. The circus' main performances would all take place under the large tent, but at the moment, the makeshift structure stood silent.

"Up just in time," Needles said. *"Circus opens to citizens of Enchanted Island tomorrow morning."*

Individual smaller tents were scattered around the open area and served as private spaces where the circus performers put on smaller shows when not dazzling the crowd under the main canopy. Each tent was decorated to give a hint as to the performer inside.

Also scattered about the vast field in between the smaller tents were magical game booths. There were games for both children and adults to participate in. My favorite was the Floating Ring Toss, where bottles gently bobbed and floated in the air, glowing softly as they drifted unpredictably. What made it even more difficult was the fact the rings could change size and shape as they sailed toward a floating bottle, making it almost impossible to win. But it was still a blast to try, especially when the vendor told me I could use my own magic to manipulate the rings to change size as well...but no matter how much of my magic I used, I still couldn't get the rings to loop around the neck of the floating bottles.

"I want to try my hand at the Enchanted Dart Throw," Needles said. *"The guy said I could use one of my quills instead of enchanted darts."*

Like the ring toss, the balloons in the dart booth floated lazily about, but it was a little easier than the ring toss, I thought. When the vendor suggested I try it out yesterday, I was able to pop a balloon on my third attempt. When the enchanted dart popped the balloon, the air shimmered, and a magical illusion revealed the prize—a stuffed phoenix that actually flew through the air. I knew Serena and Grant's one-year-old twins, Cayden and Brooke, would *love* the animal, and I couldn't wait to give it to them.

But knowing the twins like I did, I couldn't wait to see them tackle the Floating Duck Pond with gusto. Even at their tender age, they could wield magic like nothing I'd ever seen before. I knew the minute their tiny little hands got ahold of one of those enchanted wands, the floating rubber ducks wouldn't stand a change.

"As long as I don't have to go inside the Magic Mirror Maze," Zoie said, "I'll be fine."

"That thing creeps me out as well," Needles said. *"It's unnatural!"*

I snorted. "And a talking and flying porcupine *is* natural?" I winked at Zoie. "But I get it. It *is* a little creepy."

The Magic Mirror Maze was pretty much what it sounded like—a huge maze that used mirrors as portals. The only thing was, the supernatural had no idea when they stepped through the mirror where exactly they'd be transported to within the maze. It was easy to get turned around. The only way out was to answer the clues that randomly popped up and floated in the air around you. These clues told participants which mirror to step through next to find the exit.

"I'm dying to know," I said. "Is Harlow bringing her new guy to the circus?"

Zoie laughed. "She is." Then held up a finger. "But before you ask who he is, I've been sworn to secrecy. So even if you threaten to torture me, I'll never tell."

"I miss the good old days of torture and spilling guts," Needles said as he flittered between Zoie and me, his wings glowing purple and red.

I laughed. "I thought—"

The sound of raised voices cut me off. I stopped and put my finger over my lips. Both Zoie and Needles immediately went still, Needles landing on my shoulder.

"Sounds like it's coming from the office tent," I whispered.

As the voices continued to elevate—causing some circus workers to pause and glance around as well—I motioned for Zoie to follow me. Coming to a stop in front of Monte Vex's office, I raised my voice so I could be heard. "Monte? It's Agent Loci-Stone. Everything okay in there?"

The tent flap opened, and the elderly witch who owned and operated the circus stared out at me, worry etched on his wrinkled face. His widow's peak stood out even more than usual against his pale face. "Agent Loci-Stone and Detective Stone, please come in. I'm afraid we have a bit of a situation on our hands."

I stepped inside the tent, Zoie close on my heels. Two men

were squared off at each other in the middle of the tent, veins pulsing and fists flexing.

"I think we are about to have an epic battle on our hands," Needles said, his tone sounding both hopeful and excited.

I was glad only close family and friends could understand Needles when he spoke...otherwise, these men may have given Needles what he wanted. I recognized both men, having been introduced to them briefly yesterday when the circus first arrived and started to set up.

Sebastian Blackwood was the star of the circus, according to the whispers. He was a talented puppeteer, but from what I'd gathered, the fairy wasn't very popular with the other circus workers.

The other man was Grigor Stonefist, the circus' strongman. He was a troll who stood nearly six foot six inches, and I was pretty sure his muscles had muscles.

"What's going on?" I asked softly, trying to deescalate the situation before it got any more out of hand.

"What's going on?" Grigor barked. "I'll tell you what's going on. Sebastian Blackwood stole my Warhammer!"

Sebastian scoffed and rolled his eyes...managing to look both bored and insulted. "Why would I steal your Warhammer, Grigor? It's ridiculous."

I held up a hand and turned to Grigor. "Why do you think he stole your Warhammer?"

"Because," Grigor said between gritted teeth, "when I returned to my performance tent after taking a break, it was gone."

"And you automatically think *I* stole it?" Sebastian scoffed. "News flash, Grigor. I don't want your Warhammer."

Grigor's nostrils flared, and he took three panting breaths before continuing his story. "I found *this* on the ground near where the Warhammer is supposed to be!" He held out his hand for everyone to see. "It's some of Sebastian's puppet string. It proves he stole it!"

I took the thin, silk-like strand out of Grigor's massive hand and studied it for a second. Lifting it to my nose, I sniffed, then handed the string to Zoie. "Is there magic on the string, Sebastian?"

"Sure is, Princess," Needles said. *"I can smell it."*

Zoie used her magic and conjured a small evidence bag and slipped the string inside.

"Yes," Sebastian said. "I use magic in my shows. What you need to know is that I drop those strings all over the place. Everyone knows that. It doesn't prove anything. Anyone here could have picked it up and then used it to try to frame me."

"I say we take him over to Kraken Kove in the kiddie section and hold him underwater until he admits to the theft!" Needles said, his wings glowing purple and green.

I pressed my lips together so I wouldn't smile. "Could we take a look inside your performance tent, Mr. Blackwood?"

The distinguished fairy scoffed and ran his hands through his short hair. "Whatever. Do whatever you must to prove I had no hand in this."

"Maybe *you* didn't," Grigor muttered, "but I wouldn't put it past one of your creepy dolls."

"Creepy dolls?" Zoie asked.

Sebastian narrowed his eyes, and a muscle jumped in his jaw as he took a step toward Grigor. "They are not *dolls,* you ignorant troll. They are puppets."

"They're creepy," Grigor said.

2

As our group made the walk over to Sebastian Blackwood's tent, I couldn't help but notice the glances others were sending our way. Sebastian was the star of the show, and everyone knew it. I'd witnessed the narrowed glances and whispered words yesterday when Sebastian would walk by. No doubt the other performers and workers were dying to know what was going on. Even if they hadn't heard the arguing, they probably suspected something was going on by the way we were all headed in one direction toward Sebastian's tent.

"*Can't miss his tent,*" Needles said. "*Outside of The Big Top, it's the biggest one here.*"

Needles was right. The puppeteer's performance tent was by far the largest on grounds outside of The Big Top. The outside fabric was dull and heavy, making it seem as though what was inside would be dark and eerie as well.

Sebastian pulled the flap back, and we all stepped inside the darkened room. My eyes were immediately drawn to the massive stage that took up a good portion of the center. It was no wonder the tent was so large. There was seating for about twenty people. What was odd, though, was the way the temperature and atmosphere changed the minute we walked inside. There seemed to be a dark, oppressive feeling inside the silent room.

"Oh, yeah. Doesn't get much creepier than this," Needles said as he flew from my shoulder and zipped around the room.

Five life-sized puppets were all standing on the stage, except for one who was sitting. Each one was suspended by strings, but the weird thing was, the strings didn't seem to be attached to anything. They hovered in the air, not connected to the control bar as you'd expect with traditional marionettes.

"That's why he uses magic on the strings," Needles said.

"Gives it an even creepier feeling," Zoie whispered so only Needles and I would hear. "You know the puppeteer should be moving the puppets, but the strings aren't attached to anything."

Sebastian motioned theatrically around the room as Grigor and Monte both glanced about the tent.

"As you can see," the puppeteer said, "there is no Warhammer here."

Saying nothing, I strolled over to one of the life-sized figures. They were all disturbingly lifelike, with glassy eyes that seemed to follow me as I came to a stop in front of a woman dressed like a young, early-1900s schoolmarm.

"This place is…odd," Zoie whispered as she sidled up next to me.

"You can say that again, Miss Zoie," Needles said as he settled on my shoulder.

Sebastian flung his arms wide. "All my puppets are accounted for, and I think you'll agree with me that none of them appears to have dashed to Grigor's tent just to steal his Warhammer."

I arched a brow. "That's what we're here to determine, Mr. Blackwood." I motioned for Zoie to start on the other side of the stage, where two life-sized puppets' cases sat. I took the three nearest me. "I'd like to take a look inside the puppets' cases."

"This is ridiculous!" Sebastian cried.

"Says the man who obviously has something to hide," Grigor countered.

Monte sighed. "Let's just get this over with. We still have a lot of work to do before we open to the public tomorrow."

I'd just opened my second case when Zoie called my name. Shooting a glance for the three men to stay put, I hurried over to where Zoie stood, Needles still perched on my shoulder.

"Got something?" I asked.

Zoie nodded and pointed at one of the cases. Glancing down, something metallic gleamed from within. I reached in and pulled out the large object. It was heavy, and as I lifted it, I was pretty sure what it was.

"My Warhammer!" Grigor cried.

I turned to Sebastian. "Care to explain this?"

Sebastian's expression was unreadable, but a muscle in his jaw ticked as he stared at the weapon. "Someone must have planted it there to frame me."

"Why would they do that?" I asked.

"Jealousy," Sebastian snapped. "Do you know how many performers would love to see me disgraced and forced out so they could step in and take my place? I draw the biggest crowds. I keep this circus afloat." He stared hard at Monte. "But no one wants to admit that I'm the one they all come to see. I'm the *real star of this circus.*"

"And I thought I had a healthy ego," Needles snickered.

Zoie crossed her arms over her chest. "Anyone in particular who might want to set you up?"

Sebastian snorted. "I can think of plenty."

"Can you give us names?" I pressed.

Sebastian remained silent, his eyes narrowing as he looked from me to the Warhammer and back again. "Unless you plan on questioning the entire circus, I can't narrow it down for you."

"So basically he's saying he's the most hated man around." Needles shot from my shoulder and did a somersault in the air. *"I can believe it."*

"Can I have my Warhammer back?" Grigor asked.

I glanced down at the impressive weapon. "Are you going to want to file charges?"

Sebastian scoffed. "For what? I did nothing wrong, and you can't prove I did!"

Grigor shook his head, but he continued to scowl at Sebastian. "No. I will press no charges…for now. As long as it doesn't happen again."

Sebastian rolled his eyes and shook his head. "Whatever. I did nothing wrong. For all I know, *you* planted the weapon in my tent, Grigor."

Before the two men could get into a yelling match again, I stepped between the two supernaturals and handed the Warhammer to Grigor. "Take your weapon and go, please."

Grigor glared once more at Sebastian before yanking the handle out of my hand. "Watch your back, Puppeteer." With that, Grigor turned and strode out of the tent.

"Thank you for handling that for us, Agent Loci-Stone," Monte said. "I fear it could have escalated rather quickly."

I glanced once more at Sebastian and his puppets before smiling at Monte. "No problem. That's why Detective Stone and I are here. Call if you need anything else."

Once we were outside and heading away from Sebastian's eerie tent, Zoie turned to me. "Think that's the end of it?"

I snorted. "Not by a long shot."

"Buckle up! It could be a bumpy ride!" Needles said as he leaped from my shoulder.

3

The rest of the day passed fairly smoothly, but by the time I dropped Zoie off at her house in town and drove the thirty minutes to my castle…I was tired and ready to see my husband.

Alex had texted while I was dropping Zoie off to let me know he'd go ahead and make us a chicken salad for dinner. Which was fine by me. I always appreciated the nights he cooked.

Hurrying into the kitchen, I took a moment to appreciate how lucky I was to have a husband so willing to help out when needed. He must have sensed me standing there because Alex looked up from layering the salad to smile at me.

"Welcome home, wife."

I grinned and hurried over to him, kissing his cheek. "Missed you. How was your day?"

"Typical." He motioned to the wine refrigerator. "I thought maybe we'd have a glass of Riesling with our chicken salad. Want to pour?"

"Heck yeah. I could use a huge glass."

Alex laughed. "Should I ask how your day went?"

"Let's just say I'm going to need at least three pretzel rods to relax." Needles dropped near the dish I kept full for him at all times and grabbed two paws full of salty pretzels. *"Or maybe all these."*

I rolled my eyes, but as I poured us each a glass, I filled Alex in on the stolen—and then found—Warhammer. We decided to forgo sitting at the table and ate at the counter barstools instead.

"So do you think this Sebastian guy really stole the Warhammer?" Alex asked as he drained the last of his wine.

I shrugged. "I'm honestly not sure. And I guess as long as nothing else happens, Grigor is willing to let it go for now. Which is fine by me. Let them settle it in a different town."

Alex laughed. "I agree."

Needles moaned, and we turned to look at him reclining against the large bowl of chicken salad we'd shared. He patted his rotund belly and moaned again. *"Why did you let me eat so much, Princess?"*

I rolled my eyes and finished off my glass of wine. "Yes, this is somehow all *my* fault."

"As long as you're aware," Needles said.

"Are you going to see your dad tonight?" Alex asked.

"I thought about it. What do you say, Needles? Feel like flying out to see Dad?"

Needles perked up, his wings glowing green and purple. *"Like you have to ask, Princess."* He shot up off the counter. *"Let's go."*

"I'll take care of cleanup," Alex said. "Go on so you can get back in time for us to snuggle on the couch in the library."

I leaned over and kissed him. "Sounds good. Let me run and change real quick, Needles. Then I'll be ready to go."

* * *

I quickly changed into my running shoes, and five minutes later, Needles and I were jogging along the dirt path behind the castle and headed for Black Forest.

As I jogged toward Mom's cottage, I slowed to a stop when I saw her on the front porch. "Hey, Mom. Surprised you aren't out seeing Dad."

"I chatted with him earlier today. I thought I'd have a nice quiet time at home tonight." She lifted the needlepoint on her lap. "I still have a ways to go to finish GiGi and Byron's wedding present."

I strode over her stepping stones, Needles flying from my shoulder to see what Mom was working on. "What are you making for them?"

"A throw pillow with their names and wedding date." She held up the fabric for me to see. "It shouldn't take me much longer. I'd also like to make them a lap quilt if I have time."

"It's gorgeous," I said, examining the needlepoint work. "You always were amazing at this stuff."

Mom laughed. "You just couldn't sit still long enough to finish a project."

I grinned. "True."

"I think it's a real showpiece, Serenity," Needles said as he settled down on the porch railing.

"Thank you, Needles." Mom settled the embroidery hoop back on her lap. "I'll probably see you tomorrow at the circus."

"Good. I think Serena and Grant are bringing the twins, so that should be fun." I threw up a quick wave and turned back toward Black Forest as Needles flew to my shoulder. "See ya tomorrow."

I jogged back to the path and was almost to the entrance of

Black Forest when a giant ball of light barreled toward me, splitting apart right before it reached me. Dozens of fireflies giggled and chirped with excitement.

"*Is the circus fun, Princess?*"

"*Did you eat cotton candy?*"

"*Black Forest King said Zoie had her first case.*"

"*Does Zoie like the circus?*"

On and on the questions and chatter went until I stopped at the entrance of the forest in front of my favorite pine tree—his massive branches so large and weighty, they brushed the forest floor.

"Hello, Mr. Pine. How're you?"

"*Princess. Lovely to see you.*" He slowly lifted a large, weighted branch high enough for me to duck under. "*Welcome home.*"

Entering Black Forest is like achieving utopia. At least, it is for me. It's almost indescribable—the overwhelming sense of peace and tranquility mixed with the harmonious presence of the forest and the animals within. Crossing over the threshold always gave me an unexplainable surge of power—a boost of strength and physical healing. Everything about Black Forest was peaceful and grounding.

Needles leaped from my shoulder and zipped ahead of me. "*Let's go, Princess!*"

I followed Needles, jogging through the forest, jumping over logs, calling out to the wildlife, and basking in the awesomeness that was Black Forest.

Before long, we came to a clearing…and I saw him.

My dad.

The largest tree in Black Forest.

Thousands of years old, he kept watch over the forest and the island. His tree roots were four feet off the ground and extended out about twenty feet from the base of his trunk. He was nearly one hundred twenty feet around, with branches averaging thirty to forty feet. When I looked up, I couldn't see the top of him. He was majestic and powerful...and he always managed to take my breath away.

"Daughter of my Heart," Dad said, his strong voice echoing in my head. *"I have missed you. Come and sit, and we will talk."*

Laughing, I levitated myself onto one of his roots, ran down the length of him, and then wrapped my arms around his trunk for a hug before plopping down to sit at his base. "Well, the circus is in town."

Dad laughed. *"Yes. And how is that going?"*

"I could do without the clowns," Needles said as he zipped through Dad's branches. *"They're creepy. But not as creepy as the life-sized puppets."*

"What is this?" Dad asked.

I filled him in on what had happened earlier and how when we went to Sebastian's tent, he had life-sized dolls that were animated using magic...unlike the humans who used strings to control the puppets. But the fact Sebastian alluded to the strings by having them attached and going straight up into the air and not attached to anything gave the puppets a sinister, creepy vibe.

"Princess!" a tiny firefly cried as she zipped over to where I sat. *"Needles said you have cotton candy. Is that true?"*

I laughed and whipped out a snack-sized Ziploc bag from the hidden pocket of my yoga pants. "It sure is." I opened the bag and gave her a small pinch...and soon dozens of fireflies were vying for my attention.

"They will be zipping around all night, Daughter," Dad said, his chuckle reverberating in my head.

"Maybe I'll bring back some caramel popcorn on my next trip."

"We've never had that!"

"What is caramel popcorn, Princess?"

"Oh, yes! Please do!"

"I'm sure I will love it!"

"Is it better than Pop Rocks?"

Needles sighed as he landed on my shoulder. *"See what you've done, Princess? They'll follow us all the way home now, peppering us with questions about caramel popcorn."*

"Wait until I tell them about funnel cake," I joked.

4

I wanted to be at the fairgrounds an hour and a half before the doors opened at 10:00, just to make sure everything was in order. I also knew Monte was holding a mandatory meeting for all workers that I wanted to attend. Zoie hopped inside the Bronco when I pulled to a stop in front of her house, and a few minutes later, I parked in the designated circus lot, and Zoie, Needles, and I rode in on a flying carpet.

Melody Spellmoore, the owner of The Spellmoore, had graciously loaned out twenty of her flying carpets to the circus, and I never passed up on a chance to ride one. If circus goers didn't want to walk to the gate, they could take a magic carpet or choose to ride a hover cart. The hover carts sat four people, and were magically enhanced to glide through the air three feet off the ground.

When we reached the front gate, I waved at a group of ticket sellers standing around and talking, and then waited patiently as a security guard waved an actual witch's wand over Zoie and me.

"It's a good thing he didn't wand me," Needles said from my

shoulder as he patted his quills. *"My lethal weapons are attached."*

"You guys are here a little early," the security guard said. "We still have an hour and a half before the gates open."

"Early bird and all that," I joked.

We stepped through the gates and headed inside. "Hey, Shayla. Hey, Zoie," a diminutive pixie said as she zipped over to us and hovered near our shoulders, her wings glowing purple and green. "Hi, Needles." She wiggled a bag that was almost the size of her. "Me and the girls are enchanting the rings for the ring toss. We have three more bags to go before we're done." She hefted the bag a little higher. "I better run."

Without another word, she turned in the air and flew away, pink pixie dust trailing behind her. She waved to Sebastian Blackwood entering his tent, but he didn't wave back.

All around us, employees and performers were working on putting the final touches on their booths and tents. As we passed by Nathaniel Nyx's tent, I lifted a hand and waved.

"He's so cute," Zoie said of the sandy-haired escape artist.

Needles snorted as he leaped from my shoulder, his wings glowing red and orange. *"How mysterious is it for a witch to be an escape artist? All he has to do is use magic to escape!"*

As if to prove Needles correct, Nathaniel waved his hand in front of his tent, and the chains and locks barring the entrance of his tent fell away. Nodding in satisfaction, he smiled and then stepped inside.

"He's still cute," Zoie said.

I grinned. "Don't tell your father I said so, but I agree."

Zoie and I fist bumped and continued walking along the dirt path.

"It's 8:45," I said. "The mandatory meeting is at 9:15. I say we just walk around the park and make sure everything looks good until the meeting."

Grigor Stonefist strode over to his tent and bent down to lift one of the hovering boulders in front of his tent flap. Grunting, he tossed it aside so the rock now hovered above the ground two feet away. Doing the same with the other two boulders barring his entrance, he placed both of his hands on his lower back, leaned back and grunted as he popped his spine back into place before striding inside his tent.

We strolled all around the twenty acres set aside for the circus. We made sure to check that the grounds were clean as we chatted with booth workers hanging up merchandise in their carts. There were enchanted puppets, magic-infused glow wands that were mood-sensitive, shapeshifting plush toys, celestial star maps, shadowbox illusions, floating lanterns, teleporting postcards, and circus-theme enchanted jewelry. I had no doubt the kids on Enchanted Island were going to be thrilled with the treasures they'd take home as a reminder of their time at the circus.

"Look over there," Zoie said. "They finally set up the enchanted face-painting booth. I can't wait for the twins to get their faces painted."

Needles snorted as he hovered between us. *"They'll probably get leopards painted on their faces instead of bubbles, and the leopards will come to life and chase everyone to their cars."*

I laughed. "Don't even say those words aloud jokingly, Needles! We don't need that whispered out into the universe."

Monte Vex stepped out of his office tent and blew a ceremonial horn, calling everyone to The Big Top.

"Must be time for the mandatory meeting," I said as I glanced at my watch. "Yep. 9:15. Right on time."

Zoie clapped her hands in excitement. "Is it weird I'm really looking forward to this?"

I grinned. "Nope. Not weird at all. I don't remember the circus ever coming to Enchanted Island when I was a kid. I went to my first circus when I was twenty-five." I laughed at the memory. "I had just started working for PADA, and my partner at the time, Zane, insisted I experience it."

Zoie waggled her eyebrows as we followed behind performers Ariella Moonshadow and Brylee Flare toward The Big Top. "Ooh. The Fallen Angel. Now *he's* a cutie as well."

Needles scoffed and fluttered between our shoulders. *"Focus on the task at hand! All this talk of boys is making me want to yank out my quills and saw off my own ears."*

Zoie and I both laughed as Needles rolled his eyes and settled back down on my shoulder, muttering under his breath.

We strolled inside the tent, along with everyone else. Monte motioned us all forward toward the big center ring where he stood. With a flick of his wrist, confetti rained down on all of us, then disappeared before it hit the ground.

"Welcome, my family!" Monte said, tears shining in his eyes. "Come closer!"

"Where's Sebastian Blackwood?"

I turned to the person who'd spoken and smiled at Willow Casper, the mythical animal whisperer. I'd only been able to talk with her once since meeting her two days ago. Willow was a fairy who could communicate with the two unicorns and one phoenix the circus had. It wasn't a physical speaking like I could do with animals...but more a bond of feeling and understanding.

Willow slapped a hand over her mouth. "Oops. Was that out loud?"

I smiled and nodded. "Yeah, it was."

"Sorry. I just noticed he's not here is all." She glanced over her shoulder. "He usually doesn't miss these meetings. Gives him a chance to be seen and remind us all how he's the drawing act, and how the people are there to see him."

I frowned. "Really? He does that?"

"Oh, yes." The fairy shrugged her broad shoulders. "But I guess when you draw in the kind of crowds he does, you can do that."

"I feel death all around me," fortune teller Madame Seraphina muttered as she shuffled past us.

"That's because everyone has to die, Seraphina," one of the popcorn vendors called out behind me.

Zoie cleared her throat, and I could tell by the way she pressed her lips together she was trying not to smile.

"I don't see Esta, either," Willow said. "Nathaniel is standing alone over there."

I was about to see where she'd pointed when Zoie staggered into me.

"Excuse me!" Esta panted as she bumped into Zoie, causing her to bump into me. "Don't want to be late." She shifted something to her other hand as she wiped sweat from her forehead and went to stand by Nathaniel.

"There she is," Willow said.

Monte spent the next ten minutes welcoming everyone and reminding them why they have the job they do, and how it's their responsibility to give the citizens of Enchanted Island a fun and magical time. His speech left me feeling excited for the next couple days.

When Monte finished his speech and everyone was shuffling out, he caught my eye and waved me over. Motioning for Zoie to follow me, we hurried over to where Monte stood.

"Hey, Monte," I said. "That was a great speech. I'm not even an employee, and I can't wait for the gates to open."

8

"Oh, Shayla, I'm so glad I ran into you," Finn said as she stepped outside Sebastian's tent. "We're done here. Goes much faster with an extra hand. I assume you want us to take the puppets with us as well, right?"

I nodded. "Yes."

"I'll camouflage the body," Finn said. "Harlow can camouflage the puppets, but she might need help levitating out all five. Can you help real quick?"

"Of course," Zoie said.

It didn't take long for Zoie and me to help Harlow with the puppets. If anyone thought it odd that the medical examiner and forensic scientists were at the circus, no one said anything aloud. Once the body and puppets were in the van, we waved goodbye and headed back inside the fairgrounds.

A few minutes later, we were standing in front of Nathaniel Nyx's tent—escape artist extraordinaire. The tent was blue and teal and did its best to mimic water.

"He's half witch, half merman, right?" Zoie asked.

I nodded. "From what I can tell."

Needles snorted at my shoulder. *"Why would it be a surprise that a mer-witch could escape an underwater trick? Wouldn't he just use magic to escape?"*

I shrugged and entered the tent. "Only one way to find out."

The inside of Nathaniel's tent was...unsettling. Unlike the calm, tranquil look of outside, the interior was completely opposite. I immediately felt oppressed and suffocating.

"These drapes are heavy," Zoie said as she ran her finger down one of the hanging fabrics.

"I think it's supposed to give the sensation of feeling weighted and maybe dragged down," I said, taking in the rest of the tent's ambiance. "Like you're drowning."

The air inside the tent was about fifteen degrees cooler than it was outside, and there was a faint scent of saltwater in the air. Shadows rippled along the tent walls as though the entire space was submerged underwater, and the blue-green lighting from overhead orbs cast an eerie glow around the dimly lit tent.

In the center of the structure, a massive glass water tank sat, its contents swirling gently even though there was no one inside. Around the tank, chains and locks dangled from hooks, shimmering faintly with magical runes.

"Okay, I thought Sebastian's tent was unsettling," Zoie said as she glanced at the myriad mirrors hovering magically against the walls, distorting our images. "Is this a circus thing? Everything needs to feel macabre?"

A faint drip of water echoed throughout the tent, and I couldn't decide if it was annoying or ominous.

"The next show isn't for another hour," a deep male voice I recognized as belonging to Nathaniel Nyx said, his back to us.

"Come back then," his assistant, Esta Topaz, said as she handed him a robe.

"Already giving us grief," Needles grumbled. *"Don't worry, Princess."* He patted his quills. *"I'll make them talk."*

I chuckled. "Hopefully, it won't come to that." I raised my voice. "Excuse me."

Nathaniel and Esta both turned around.

Nathaniel had sandy-blond hair, sea-green eyes, and the athletic build of a merman. The few times I'd run into him, he was quick with a smile and a joke. I guessed him to be in his thirties.

Esta Topaz had long dark hair that hung down her back in waves, and her big brown eyes had a hint of innocence in them that the circus life hadn't diminished. She wasn't nearly as friendly as Nathaniel…but I thought it was because she was shy, not purposely standoffish.

"Oh, I'm sorry." Nathaniel flashed us a smile. "I didn't know it was you guys." He finished belting his robe and strode toward us, Esta behind him. "What's up?"

"We need to talk," I said.

Nathaniel snorted. "It sounds like you're going to break up with me." When no one cracked a smile, he frowned. "Okay. Talk about what?"

"Sebastian Blackwood," I said.

Nathaniel rolled his eyes. "What about him? In case no one's told you, we're not exactly friends."

"And why is that?" Zoie asked.

Nathaniel cocked his head and crossed his arms over his chest. "Can I ask why it's any of your business?"

"Yeah," Esta added. "Whatever Sebastian said about us, it's not true."

Nathaniel held up his hand. "Don't say anything else, Esta. Not until we know why they're asking about Sebastian."

I stepped forward. I didn't have time to dance around

Nathaniel's ego. "I know I was introduced to you as the game warden of Enchanted Island, but before I was the game warden, I was a detective for over fifteen years with PADA."

Nathaniel's eyes went wide. "PADA? What the heck does PADA want with me? I'm not wanted for a crime!"

"We'll see about that," Needles snickered.

"And my full title is actually Detective Zoie Stone," Zoie said. "I'm also with PADA."

This time, Nathaniel looked impressed. "Seriously? What are you, twenty?"

One corner of Zoie's mouth lifted in a small smile. "Eighteen, actually."

Nathaniel whistled. "Impressive. But, again, I don't know what PADA wants with me."

"We want to talk about Sebastian Blackwood," I said, motioning to one of the seats. "Why don't we sit down?"

The four of us sat while Needles settled on my shoulder.

"We have another show in forty-five minutes," Esta said. "Just so you know."

"We'll be done way before then," I promised. "I'll start with you, Nathaniel. Tell me about your relationship with Sebastian Blackwood."

Nathaniel frowned. "Does this have anything to do with Ariella coming to my tent a while ago, claiming something was going on over at Sebastian's tent?"

I nodded. "It does."

When I said nothing else, Nathaniel sighed, folded his arms over his chest, and leaned back in his seat. "I was his understudy for about four years. I was hired to take care of the puppets and learn the magic and the skits. This way, if Sebastian was sick, or if Monte wanted to add another rotation to the schedule, he could."

"And did you learn from Sebastian?" I asked.

Nathaniel snorted and rolled his eyes. "As much as one can. Let's just say he's difficult to work with. I don't know if you've talked to him much in the two days you've been around, but Sebastian Blackwood is a narcissistic jerk—and that's me being nice."

"So you worked with him for four years?" Zoie asked.

"Yep, and then when I pushed to have more time in the spotlight to showcase my abilities with the puppets, Sebastian put an immediate stop to it. He ended up telling Monte that either I had to be reassigned or he'd quit. And it wasn't hard to figure out which side Monte would take. Sebastian draws in quite the crowd."

"So we've heard," I said. "How'd you get to be the escape artist?"

Nathaniel chuckled. "The previous escape artist, Luna, ended up marrying one of the clowns, believe it or not. She decided to join her husband in his act, opening up this performance tent. She wasn't a merperson, so her escapism was different. I escape from water because I'm part merman."

"And when Monte told Nathaniel about me being half mermaid," Esta cut in, looking adoringly at Nathaniel, "Nathaniel asked me to join him."

Nathaniel smiled at Esta and patted her hand. "That's right."

"Lovers?" Needles mused.

"And you, Esta?" Zoie asked, turning to face the assistant. "How long have you worked for the circus?"

"About six years," Esta said. "I worked four years over in the kiddie area in the mermaid lagoon." She beamed up at Nathaniel. "Then Nathaniel asked me to join him."

"But what do all these questions have to do with Sebastian?" Nathaniel asked. "I still don't understand why you're here."

I leaned forward and stared into Nathaniel's green eyes. "Earlier this morning, the body of Sebastian Blackwood was found in his tent. It looked like he'd been strangled with his own puppet strings."

Esta gasped and Nathaniel's eyes went huge.

"Seriously?" Nathaniel said. "Sebastian is dead?" He thought about that for a moment and smiled. "Well, I'm sorry for Monte, and it might hurt his bottom line, but I can't say I'm sorry. Like I said, the guy was a jerk."

"And did you decide that jerk needed to die?" Needles mused.

"I need to know where you both were from 8:30 to 9:30," I said.

"We were both here," Esta said.

Nathaniel nodded. "Yep. I think we arrived at the tent around 8:40 or so. I say that because we left the group camp around 8:30. So I think saying it took us ten minutes to get to our performance tank sounds right. Then we came in and just did warmups."

"What does that mean?" Zoie asked.

"I make sure all our props are working properly," Esta said.

"And I practice free-range. Meaning I do the stunts without the props at first because Esta is checking everything."

I nodded. "And you both did that from 8:45 until you left for the meeting at 9:15?"

The two glanced quickly at each other, and something passed between them.

"Well," Nathaniel hedged, "this morning was a little different, to be honest."

"I forgot a prop at my home tent," Esta said. "We noticed yesterday when practicing that a garment clasp was loose. So I brought the jacket back with me last night to darn and fix. Only I forgot to bring it this morning. So I told Nathaniel I'd just meet him at The Big Top."

I thought about the water on the ground in Sebastian's tent. "Were you both in the water this morning?"

"Yes," they responded simultaneously.

Zoie turned to Nathaniel. "Did anyone come inside the tent after Esta left?"

"Absolutely not," Nathaniel said briskly. "No one is allowed to see how the tricks are done."

Zoie frowned. "So there's no one who can corroborate you were in your tent here from 9:00 until 9:15?"

Nathaniel narrowed his eyes at her. "I guess not."

"And you," I said, motioning to Esta. "Did you stop and talk to anyone on your walk to the encampment? Maybe see Willow?"

Esta's brows furrowed. "No. I didn't have time, to be honest. It's a couple minutes to the campsite. I was almost running back as it was, so I wouldn't be late for the meeting."

Zoie nodded. "I remember you accidently ran into me as Monte was about to start the meeting."

"Yeah," Esta said, smiling. "Sorry about that."

I crossed my arms over my chest. "Do you know of anyone who may have been angry at Sebastian?"

Nathaniel snorted. "Who wasn't? The guy never talked to anyone unless it was to yell at them."

"Anyone in particular come to mind?" Zoie asked.

I could have sworn I saw a flash of something in his eyes, but it was gone just as quickly. "Nope. No one comes to mind."

I had the distinct impression he was lying to me, but I wasn't surprised. From what I understood, the supernatural circus people were a family in and of themselves. They didn't care for outsiders much, and if it meant protecting one of their own, they probably would do it.

"Okay, you two," I said, standing and waiting for Zoie to stand as well. "Thank you for your time. We'll let you get back to your downtime."

Nathaniel pursed his lips and looked toward the entrance of his tent. "I take it everyone knows?"

I shook my head. "No. You two are the first people we've spoken to."

"Why us?" Esta demanded.

"It's just where we stopped," I lied.

No way was I going to throw Monte under the bus, or tell them about the water we found in Sebastian's tent.

Nathaniel stared up at me, like he was trying to assess how truthful I'd just been. "Well, good luck with your investigation." He stood slowly as well, so Esta leaped to her feet. "Now, if you'll excuse us, Esta and I should get back to our jobs. With Sebastian dead, Monte may need me to do a couple more shows in his place."

"And another motive to want Sebastian dead," Needles said.

"And me too?" Esta said hopefully. "I could probably do a routine alone. I've been training for a while now."

Nathaniel gave her a tight smile. "And maybe you as well, Esta. You've earned it."

"Is it my imagination," Needles mused as we headed for the front of the tent, *"or does Nathaniel sound a little fake with his praise?"*

9

"Are we seeing Ariella Moonshadow next?" Zoie asked as we stepped outside Nathaniel Nyx's tent.

I nodded as Needles flew from my shoulder and zipped toward the pretzel stand. *"Princess, I'm about to starve to death!"*

I rolled my eyes as Zoie laughed. "Fine. I'll get you one now if it means you stop whining."

Needles turned mid-air and glared at me. *"A warrior never whines, Princess!"*

"Could have fooled me," I muttered to Zoie…but low enough Needles didn't hear.

"I heard that! You forget our connection, Princess?"

Zoie giggled, but wisely kept her mouth closed.

I paid for the massive salted pretzel and handed it to Needles. It was bigger than him, and it required him to hold it with two paws as he chowed down, flying between Zoie and me as we headed toward Ariella's performance tent.

"Her tent is beautiful," Zoie said, lightly running her hand over the material.

The outside of the tent was midnight blue with silver twinkling stars and a bright full moon near the top. I'd seen the celestial witch around, and she seemed friendly and popular. I couldn't help but wonder why her name was mentioned in connection with Sebastian's death.

The sign on the tent said a show was in progress, but according to my watch, it was due to end in five minutes. I wasn't in that big of a hurry, so I figured we could people-watch for a few minutes.

Needles lifted his head from his giant pretzel and used it to point to the left. *"Incoming!"*

Zoie and I turned to see what he was talking about.

"It's GiGi and some of her friends!" Zoie exclaimed.

I smiled as my octogenarian grandmother strolled down the dirt path with two of her coven witches, the equally elderly Gertrude Anise and Hagatha Broomly.

The three witches looked excited and full of mischief.

"Good morning, granddaughter," GiGi said as she leaned over and kissed my cheek. "Zoie, lovely to see you." GiGi gave Zoie a hug before turning to Needles, who'd gone back to chowing down on his pretzel. "And Needles, staying out of trouble this morning?"

Needles lifted his head, a ring of salt outlining his mouth, his wings glowing red and purple. *"Never!"*

GiGi laughed and told the two witches with her what he'd said.

"Are you waiting to see the aerialist perform?" Gertrude Anise asked.

"Don't be silly, Gertrude," GiGi said. "Shayla and Zoie are working this weekend. They are making sure the grounds don't get damaged or destroyed." GiGi frowned and narrowed her eyes at me. "What are you two doing standing here next to this tent?"

"Always with the questions," I joked, hoping to redirect the conversation elsewhere.

GiGi met and held my gaze. My grandmother was not a fool. She knew something was up.

"Where's Byron?" I asked, trying once again to divert her attention.

GiGi was getting married in three months to Byron Sealy, a selkie shifter, and I couldn't be happier. Where GiGi could be stubborn and bossy…Byron was laid-back and easy-going. They were a perfect match for each other.

Hagatha Broomly placed a withered hand to her chest. "He went to get us some cotton candy and popcorn. Isn't he a doll?"

"I thought he was a seal," Needles joked as he shoved the last of his pretzel inside his mouth.

GiGi narrowed her eyes at Needles. "Watch yourself, Porcupine."

Luckily, before Needles could respond, Ariella's tent flap opened, and a crowd of people meandered out, causing us all to step aside so we wouldn't get trampled.

"Where's the puppeteer?" Gertrude asked, looking around. "The map says his tent is around here somewhere."

She held up a paper map that had been enchanted with magical ink to show glowing lines of where tents, booths, and food stations were located. The map was constantly changing to display the next show times for each tent and the quickest route to get there from where the person holding the map was standing. It was actually quite clever magic, and when I had asked Monte who enchanted the maps, he'd beamed and said he had.

"Where are you guys heading to next?" I asked, hoping to send them on their way.

"I want to check out the fortune teller," Gertrude said.

Zoie laughed. "You guys better go before she gets booked up."

"Quite right, dear," Gertrude said.

"Oh, look," Hagatha added. "Here comes Byron with our snacks now. We better go, girls."

GiGi was still scrutinizing me, and it was all I could do not to squirm under her knowing gaze. "What time is your mom coming tonight?"

"I think she, Serena, Grant, and the twins are all coming around 4:00," I said. "What about Aunt Starla and Walt?"

"Your Aunt Starla isn't feeling well, so she and Walt aren't going to make it. But I promised lots of pictures," GiGi said. "If Byron and I are still here, I'll look for you all."

We waved goodbye and turned back to the tent, ready to go inside now that it was empty.

"Do you think GiGi suspects something's up?" Zoie asked.

I laughed. "Oh, yeah."

"Nothing gets by the dragon lady," Needles said.

I pushed aside the flap to the entrance and stepped into Ariella Moonshadow's tent. It was immediately clear the celestial witch used glamour in her performances. From the outside, the tent looked no taller than six feet, but the minute you walked inside, it was more like twelve feet high.

The lighting inside was a soft moonlight glow with silvery streaks that streamed across the air near the roof of the tent, where various constellations flickered randomly. I smiled at the orbs of light that meandered slowly around the room like small floating moons.

There were long strands of shimmering silks in shades of violet, silver, and blue that hung from the ceiling, and in the center of the tent, a pair of glowing rings floated magically in the air.

I hadn't seen Ariella's performance yet, but I'd heard whispers of how she used her celestial magic to make it seem as though she was defying gravity, almost bending the air as she moved.

Ariella stepped out from behind a curtain and let out a little squeak...then laughed self-consciously. "Sorry! You guys startled me." Her fiery red hair was pulled back in a tight bun at the nape of her neck, and crescent moons dangled from her lobes. "I'm so glad you're here, though. Brylee and I are so worried. Do you know what's going on? No one has seen Sebastian all morning, and I know his tent isn't up."

"You and Sebastian are friends?" I mused, not having to fake the surprise in my voice.

Ariella's hazel eyes flashed, but I couldn't detect the emotion. "Sort of."

"What does that mean?" Needles demanded from my shoulder.

"You didn't see him before the mandatory meeting?" I asked.

Ariella shook her head and placed her hands on her flat stomach, her teal leotard standing out from her pale skin. "No. And I've got a bad feeling in the pit of my stomach. There's no reason for Sebastian's tent not to be where it's supposed to be on opening day. Can you please tell me what's going on?"

I nodded. "Of course. I'm sorry to inform you, Ariella, but Sebastian Blackwood's body was found this morning in his tent."

Ariella's mouth dropped. "*What?* Are you saying...are you telling me Sebastian's dead? Like, *really* dead?"

"Well, he's not fake dead," Needles said.

"Yes," I said. "I'm sorry for your loss."

"How?" she croaked as she bent over at the waist. "Can I sit down?"

"Of course," Zoie said. "I'm sure this is shocking."

Ariella dropped down into a vacant chair and nodded as she closed her eyes. "I just need a minute."

Zoie and I sat down as well, and when she finally composed herself and opened her eyes, I smiled gently. "We're sorry for your loss."

"How did he die?" she asked.

"We are still waiting on the autopsy," I said. "But I can tell you he was found with some of his strings wrapped around his neck."

Ariella gasped. "He was strangled?"

I shrugged. "Like I said, the autopsy isn't in yet."

"Do the local police know?" she demanded. "Shouldn't someone be here asking questions? And should the circus still be open?"

I held up my hand to stop her barrage of questions. "Zoie is a full-time detective with PADA, and I—"

"Wait. *Seriously?*" Ariella leaned forward to stare at Zoie. "You're a detective with PADA?"

Zoie smiled. "I am. And Shayla worked as a PADA detective for over fifteen years. So we are more than qualified to handle the investigation."

"I guess you are," Ariella whispered. "Wow. And yet you two are working as groundkeepers for the circus?"

I grinned. "Something like that." I shifted in my chair. "Back to Sebastian. You two were friends?"

"Yes. I mean, I know what people said about Sebastian, and for the most part, they're right. He was…" She gave a self-deprecating laugh. "He was awful. He could be harsh and cruel and cutting." She smiled wistfully. "But when he was kind, he could be very charismatic."

"You were in a relationship with Sebastian." I didn't pose it as a question. It was obvious by the look on her face the two were or had once been in a relationship.

"Chicks always dig the bad boys," Needles said. *"It's why I have to beat them back with my quills."*

Zoie coughed so she wouldn't laugh aloud.

Ariella nodded. "We were, yes. For almost a year." She wiped away a tear. "We broke up about two weeks ago. Totally him. I was blindsided, and I didn't take it well."

"Maybe he spelled her," Needles suggested. *"Why else would a sweet girl like her date Sebastian?"*

Ariella jumped up from the chair and walked over to a purple silk that had been dropped down from the ceiling. She wrapped her right hand around the silk and leaned her head against the material. "Have you told Brylee?"

Zoie glanced at me, but I gave a small shake of my head. I didn't want to know why everyone was curious about Brylee Flare until I had a chance to speak with her.

"Not yet," I said. "She's next on our list. Can you tell me the last time you saw or spoke to Sebastian?"

Ariella nodded and looked up toward the ceiling, as though in thought, and her body swayed against the silk. "To actually see and talk with him? Last night. I saw him in front of his tent down at the campsites. He was really angry about what happened with Grigor. I stopped and told him I didn't think it was true. I didn't believe for one second he stole the Warhammer, but he didn't want to hear from me. He yelled at me and told me to go away."

"What time was that?" I asked.

Ariella shrugged and kicked her legs up in the air, reaching her left hand high and grasping the silk. Her body looked like it was at a perfect ninety-degree angle. "Maybe right before dinner? Like around five?"

I felt a shift in the air, and I knew Ariella was using magic to climb up the rope, which surprised me. As an aerialist, surely she could climb the rope easily enough? I could understand using magic maybe to bend and manipulate the air as she glided through it to enhance the experience…but to need magic to move seemed unnecessary.

"Did you see Sebastian this morning?" Zoie asked.

Ariella shook her head. She was now about ten feet off the ground, still at a ninety-degree angle. "No. I mean, I saw him walk into his tent when most of us walked to ours as well this morning, but I didn't say anything to him."

"Was the breakup amicable?" I asked.

Ariella let out a snort of laughter. "No. I wasn't kidding when I said I was totally blindsided when Sebastian said he wanted to break up. Gave me some song and dance about focusing more time on his act." She snorted again. "He'd been a puppeteer here for over twenty-five years. That man could perform his skits in his sleep." She sighed and rested her head against the silk. "He just couldn't come up with a better lie."

I was about to ask another question when Ariella seemed to lose her grip on the silk. She started to fall, reaching out blindly for the silk…but before I could stand and whisper a spell to help her, she caught herself with her own spell. Once again, the air shifted, and she stopped just short of the ground.

She gave a small, scared, almost embarrassed laugh. "Oops. I seem to have lost my grip." She stood and brushed herself off. "I guess I better focus on one thing at a time."

I looked down and noticed her right hand was fisted. "Are you okay, Ariella?"

She nodded and flexed her right hand. "I need to drink more

water and eat more bananas. Sometimes my hand cramps up on me."

"Be sure to take care of yourself, Ariella," Zoie said. "Where were you this morning between 8:30 and 9:30?"

"Way to keep her on her toes, Miss Zoie," Needles said, his wings glowing purple and green.

"Me?" Ariella pressed a hand to her chest. "This morning? Well, I was up here making sure my ropes and everything were secure. I did a couple of practices, and then when I noticed it was 9:15, I went outside and looked around for Brylee. She'd mentioned wanting to walk over to The Big Top together."

"Again with Brylee," Needles murmured.

"And did you meet up with Brylee?" Zoie asked.

Ariella nodded. "Yes. We walked to the meeting together, listened to Monte's pep talk, and then we left."

"One last thing," I said. "Do you know of anyone who might have been angry enough with Sebastian to want him dead?"

Like Nathaniel Nyx, I saw something flash in Ariella's eyes. Did both of them know someone but didn't want to say? I was about to push when Ariella shook her head.

"No, sorry," she said. "I don't know anyone who would be angry enough to murder Sebastian."

"Did anyone come into your tent this morning while you were practicing?" I asked.

Ariella frowned and shook her head. "No. I don't like distractions when warming up. Why?"

I shook my head. "No reason. I just wondered if anyone could corroborate you were in your tent the entire time."

Ariella's mouth dropped, and anger flashed in her eyes. "I can assure you I was! And I didn't kill Sebastian!"

"That's what they all say, Princess," Needles said sarcastically.

"Thank you, Ariella," I said. "I'm sorry for your loss. You seem to have truly cared for Sebastian."

Ariella let out a soft laugh. "For all the good it did me. But, yeah, I did. Thank you."

"I like your earrings," Zoie said.

Ariella smiled and flicked one of the moons. "Thank you. They were a gift from Sebastian."

We said goodbye and headed out of the tent.

10

"I'm hungry," Needles said the minute we stepped out of Ariella's tent. *"Time for lunch."*

"You just had a pretzel!" I exclaimed.

"That was just a snack, Princess."

Zoie chuckled. "Are we going to go talk to Brylee Flare next?"

I nodded. "Yes. I'm ready to have my questions answered."

"I suppose I'll just die of starvation," Needles grumbled from my shoulder as he wrapped his red and gray wings around his body in what I knew was a pout.

Brylee Flare's performance tent was adorned with deep red and orange fabrics that seemed to shimmer like embers in the fading light. Flames danced along the edges of the tent, flickering in rhythmic patterns. Intricate symbols of flames and phoenix feathers were stitched into the fabric, glowing faintly as if ignited by an internal, magical spark.

There was a wall of enchanted flames barring the entrance to the tent flap and a sign hovering inside the flames.

"According to the sign," Zoie said, "her next performance isn't for another hour."

"Maybe she's at the encampment having lunch," I mused. "Let's go see if she's down there."

We'd just passed The Big Top and skirted around the back when I came across Willow Casper caring for the phoenix and two unicorns.

"Hey, guys," she called out. "You just missed these three beauties perform inside." She rested her head against one of the unicorns and patted his flank. "Such crowd pleasers."

"I bet," I said, stepping closer to the animals.

"I'm too hot for my own good," a female voice said in a teasing tone.

I glanced over at the fiery-red phoenix who had spoken and laughed.

"What?" Willow asked.

"I was laughing at what your phoenix just said," I said by way of explanation.

"Blaze," the phoenix said.

"Blaze." I nodded. "I like it."

"I'm Zephyr," the male unicorn said, *"and this is my mate, Aurora."*

"It's lovely to meet you, Zephyr and Aurora," I said.

"Wow," Willow whispered. "I know you said you could communicate with animals, but to actually see it happen in person is amazing."

"I envy her ability too," Zoie said.

The roar of the crowd inside The Big Top drew me back to my current assignment. "Listen, Willow. I have a quick question. This morning, around 9:00, did you happen to see Esta Topaz run by here? She may have been heading toward the encampment.

She said she forgot a garment for Nathaniel's show and ran to her tent to get it."

Willow pressed her lips together and glanced upward. "No, can't say I did. But I was also busy with my gang here." She gave Zephyr another pat. "Had to make sure they looked beautiful for their debut today."

"I didn't see her, either," Aurora said.

"I was meditating while Zephyr was getting groomed," Blaze said, *"so I wasn't paying much attention. But I don't remember seeing her, either."*

"Is this about the whispers regarding Sebastian Blackwood?" Willow asked. "I don't think anyone knows exactly what's going on, but there's a lot of speculation."

I nodded. "Yes, this has to do with Sebastian." I was about to say goodbye when I thought of something else. "What about Brylee Flare? Did you see her at any time this morning?"

"I know Brylee," Blaze said. *"I have a soft spot for her. We are both born of the fire. She sometimes visits me, and I've given her one of my feathers for her tent. She is nice and treats me kindly."*

I held up my hand when I noticed Willow was going to answer my question about Brylee. "One minute, please, Willow." I strolled closer to the phoenix, marveling at her beauty. *"What can you tell me about Brylee with regard to Sebastian Blackwood? Do you know him?"*

"I don't know him personally," Blaze said. *"But I know Brylee knows him and doesn't like him, so I don't like him, either."* The bird rose a couple feet higher in the air and spread her wings…her red and orange feathers making her look like she was on fire. *"I saw them arguing."*

"Brylee and Sebastian?" Needles asked.

"*Yes,*" Blaze said. "*Two moons ago on our first night here. I was restless, so I went flying.*"

"*What did they argue about?*" I mused. "*Could you hear?*"

"*Yes. Because I didn't like the way Sebastian was yelling at Brylee, I dropped down for a closer look. If he got physical with her, I was going to show him just how hot my fire can be when I aim it at something.*"

Needles chuckled. "*And did you have to scorch him any?*"

Blaze shook her head. "*No. Brylee was holding her own. My friend was demanding Sebastian help pay for her mom's medical bills since he had a lot of money.*" Blaze paused. "*She then said something I didn't understand. Something about rumors and how he got the extra money by evil means or something like that. I didn't understand it. But then Sebastian laughed and said the only way Brylee would get money for her mom's medical bills would be over his dead body.*"

Needles cleared his throat but said nothing.

"What did Brylee say?" I asked.

Blaze was silent.

"I know Brylee is your friend," I said, "but I really need to know what happened next."

Blaze lowered herself to the ground, no longer glowing red and orange. "*Brylee said she could make that happen. And then she raised her hands and shot a ball of fire at him. He laughed and batted it aside and said she was just like her mother. Brylee then ran away. I was going to go after her, but I got the feeling she wanted to be alone.*"

"Thank you, Blaze," I said. "That's helpful."

I turned back to Willow. "I need to go. Hopefully, I'll run across Brylee down at her encampment tent."

Willow shook her head. "Brylee won't be down there. If she has a minute free, she'll be visiting her mom."

Zoie frowned. "Her mom is here at the circus?"

Tears filled Willow's eyes as she nodded. "Yes. Though I'm not sure for how much longer."

"Where's her mom?" I asked.

"In the infirmary," Willow said.

11

I quickly filled Zoie in on what Blaze had told Needles and me as we hurried toward the infirmary.

"Who is Brylee Flare?" Zoie mused. "And why is her mom in the infirmary? I have so many questions regarding this mysterious woman."

"You're not the only one." I waved at citizens and regulars I recognized from Serena's and Tamara's bakery.

Because the infirmary was on the other side of the circus, it would take about ten minutes for us to get there with the crowd. We were almost at the hospital tent when Madame Seraphina stepped in front of me.

The fortune teller raised a withered, shaking hand and pointed a finger at me. "Stay away from the porcupine. He will attack you! You will bleed!" She pointed to her forehead. "I saw it happen."

Before I could react, Needles leaped from my shoulder, his wings glowing black and red as he pulled two quills out of his back, one in each paw. He whipped them through the air as he zipped toward her.

"*Take it back right now, Witch! Blasphemy! How dare you say such lies! I would never hurt the Princess!*"

Madame Seraphina drew back as Needles continued to whip his quills through the air.

"Needles," I admonished. "I'm sure she didn't mean anything by it."

"I meant every word of it," Madame Seraphina said.

"She just doesn't know when to stop," Zoie hissed.

I had to get ahold of the situation before Needles combusted from outright fury.

"You said this morning you felt death around you," I said to Madame Seraphina. "What did you mean?"

Madame Seraphina gave Needles a speculative glance before turning back to me. "I only say what I feel and see, usually with my third eye."

"*I'm about to carve out that third eye, Witch!*" Needles muttered as he threw down his quills and zipped back to my shoulder, his wings still glowing bright red.

"Did you know whose death you felt?" I asked Madame Seraphina.

The old witch narrowed her eyes and shook her head. "Not at the time, but I have since heard the whispers."

"Can you see who committed the murder?" Zoie asked.

Madame Seraphina shook her head. "No, child. My gift does not work that way. Just because I am a seer does not mean I actually *see* death."

"*I'd like to make it so she sees* her *death,*" Needles muttered from my shoulder.

"Thank you, Madame Seraphina," I said.

"Heed my warning." She glared at Needles. "Stay away from the porcupine!"

Before Needles could chase after her, I ran my hand soothingly over his head. "It's okay, Needles. We all know you would never hurt me. Sometimes seers don't understand exactly what it is they are feeling or seeing."

"She made it sound like I would hurt you, Princess. I would rather cut off my quills than raise one in harm to you."

I raised my shoulder high enough so that Needles was close to my cheek. Turning my head, I kissed the side of his face. "I know you would never do anything to hurt me."

Zoie glanced over to where the seer had moved off to. "What do you suppose the old witch meant by all of that? She'd never have said it if she knew Needles."

"Exactly," I said. "Let's put it out of our minds and go question Brylee Flare. I want to know her relationship with Sebastian Blackwood, and why she thinks Sebastian should pay for her mother's medical bills."

When we reached the infirmary tent, I wasn't surprised to see we could walk right in. Since a majority of Enchanted Island supernaturals were fairies or witches and had the ability to do magic to heal small wounds or anything else that might arise while at the circus, I wasn't sure what the infirmary was for… until I noticed the patients inside the tent were all circus workers.

A pixie zipped over to us, purple pixie dust leaking from a wing. "Hello. How can I help you?"

"We need to see Brylee Flare and her mother," I said.

The pixie's wings stopped fluttering, and she drifted down to a nearby table. "Can I ask why? Tika is *very* sick." The little pixie looked over her shoulder, then leaned in. "And I do mean *very* sick." Tears filled her eyes. "I'm not sure how much longer she can hold on."

"I'm so sorry," I said. "But I'm afraid it's important I speak to them. I'm Agent Loci-Stone, and this is Detective Stone."

Fear and something else passed over the little pixie's face, but she quickly schooled her features. "Of course. Follow me, please."

She took off toward the back of the enormous tent, and Zoie and I quickly followed. There were small curtained-off areas where witches and fairies were administering medical aid to workers.

When the pixie paused outside a curtained room, she turned to us, her wings glowing blue and gray. "Tika and Brylee are both inside. Please go easy on them. They're under a lot of stress right now. If you need anything else, my name is Vaida."

"Thank you, Vaida." I waited for the pixie to fly away, blue pixie dust leaking from her as she zipped back toward the front of the tent. Pulling the curtain aside, I stepped inside the room—Needles still on my shoulder and Zoie right behind me.

"What's the meaning of this?" Brylee Flare demanded as she stood and turned toward us. "Can't you see I'm with my mom?"

I glanced down at the frail elemental witch lying in the bed, and my heart squeezed. It was plain to see the woman was barely hanging on to life.

12

"I'm sorry to disturb you," I said. "But I'm Agent Loci-Stone, and this is Detective Stone. We need to speak to you both."

Brylee frowned. "What about?"

"It's about Sebastian Blackwood," I said.

"May he rot," Tika whispered.

I glanced quickly at Zoie. Was Tika saying she knew he was dead already? How would she and Brylee have known? Could it be that Ariella Moonshadow got to Brylee before we did?

"So you know about Sebastian?" I asked.

"That he's a despicable fairy?" Tika mused. "Yes. I knew the moment he tossed me aside twenty-six years ago."

I shook my head. "No, that he's dead."

Both women gasped and clasped hands.

"Good!" Brylee said.

I cocked my head and stared at Brylee. "Can you tell me the relationship between you and Sebastian?"

"We didn't have a relationship," Brylee hissed.

"Were you related?" Zoie mused. "Or maybe more than acquaintances?"

Brylee raised her lip in disgust. "Gross! That no-good loser was my father!"

"Now it's starting to make sense," Needles said.

"Sebastian Blackwood was your father," I said slowly. "That accounts for you being half celestial witch and half fairy."

"I try not to acknowledge the fairy half of me," Brylee said.

"Even still," Zoie said, "we're sorry for your loss."

"Why?" Brylee hissed. "I'm not. I'm actually—"

"Stay calm, Brylee," Tika whispered, cutting off whatever Brylee was going to say.

Brylee closed her eyes and breathed in and out before opening her eyes once again. "There's no need for your condolences." She folded her arms across her chest. "He never once acknowledged me or my mom, for that matter."

"I'm getting motive-to-kill up to my eyeballs," Needles said.

"I hope you don't mind me asking, Tika," I said. "The nurse said you're very sick. I can see that for myself." I motioned around the room. "Why are you here?"

Tika patted her daughter's hand. "I'm dying. It's a fact. I have Infernal Decay. My organs are slowly burning and dying. Usually prevalent in fire elemental witches." A tear slid down her cheek, and Brylee leaned over to wipe it away. "I'm here because Monte promised I would always have a place here. Me and Brylee."

Brylee yanked two tissues from a box and handed one to her mom, then wiped her own eyes with her tissue. "You don't have to talk about this, Mom. Save your strength."

Tika closed her eyes and sighed. "I'll have plenty of time to rest shortly, Brylee." She opened her eyes and looked at me. "Monte and I go way back. He's sort of like my adopted dad.

When he first opened the circus all those years ago, it was just me and Sebastian as his crowd drawers." She gave me a small smile. "We didn't make any money our first year. But it drew us all together—Sebastian and me especially." More tears trailed down her cheeks, and Brylee helped wipe them away. "We'd just celebrated a year and a half open when I discovered I was pregnant. Unfortunately, Sebastian wasn't the settling down kind of fairy. Only I didn't know it until it was too late."

"As my mom said," Brylee hissed, "may he rot."

It looked like Tika was about to chastise her daughter, but either she didn't have the strength, or she thought her daughter was right and let it go. "When Monte found out I was pregnant, he assured me I would always have a place in his circus. Being pregnant didn't prohibit me from working my fire-enhanced act, so I stayed on. For many years, I thought Sebastian might one day change his mind and embrace Brylee and me. But he never did."

I glanced over Brylee. "Brylee, I need to ask you where you were this morning from 8:30 to 9:30."

Brylee gestured around the room. "Here. I got here at 7:00 and didn't leave until I had to go to the mandatory meeting."

"What time did you leave the infirmary?" I asked.

"I don't know. I think I left around 8:45. I remember the new shift was starting to come on."

"Ariella said she met Brylee at her tent, and then they walked over, Princess," Needles said.

I nodded. "It took us ten minutes to walk to the infirmary, and that's only because of the crowd," I said. "If you left here at 8:45 and met up with Ariella right before the 9:15 meeting, that leaves you a little over twenty minutes to account for."

Brylee huffed and threw her hands in the air. "Seriously? You want me to account for twenty minutes? I don't know. Maybe I walked extra slow? Maybe I stopped and meditated in the woods for a few minutes? I can't remember." She gestured to her mom, fire in her eyes. "I've got a mother who may not live for another day or two without immediate intervention. You seriously think I can account for twenty minutes with everything going on?"

It would have been a good speech had I not seen her poking around down by Sebastian's private tent earlier this morning.

"Think back to when the gates were about to open," I said.

"What?" Brylee demanded.

I gave her a small smile. "I saw you down at the encampment. You were near Sebastian's tent. Can you tell me why?"

"Well, I didn't know he was dead, if that's what you're asking. I just figured I'd go down to his tent while he was working."

"Why?" Zoie asked.

Brylee sighed. "There were always rumors Sebastian used his puppets to steal, and I wanted to know if it was true."

"Why after all this time?" I pressed.

"Because he should be helping to pay for some of Mom's treatments! It's not like the potions and ingredients for the potions are free, you know? Monte won't tell me how much of a bill I've racked up, but I'm sure it's huge. Monte is covering a lot of the cost. That lowlife Sebastian should pay for something! He never paid any child support or helped Mom and me in any way."

"Oh, Brylee," Tika said. "You shouldn't waste your energy on him."

"Which leads me to my next question," I said. "Do you know who inherits now that Sebastian is dead?"

Brylee and Tika glanced at each other before Brylee snorted. "I doubt it's me." She shrugged. "I have no idea. But you can bet I'm going to ask that person for a loan the minute I find out."

"Brylee," Tika whispered. "You aren't going into more debt for me. My time is up. The potions are only prolonging my life a little at a time. There's no cure."

Brylee grasped her mom's hand. "It's time I can have with you!"

Another tear slipped down Tika's cheek. "I know. But the cost is just too great."

"Tell me about the thefts," I said. "Why do you think Sebastian was stealing?"

Brylee shrugged. "I don't know if it's true or not, but there were always whispers that he may have used his puppets to steal from circus attendees. He'd always set his puppets outside his tent after his show in the evenings, and people would flock to them. He could have used magic and had any one of them lift a wallet or something without notice. I wanted to know if it was true, and if it was, I wanted a cut of it." She glanced down at her mom. "We deserve it."

"Not like that, Brylee," her mom whispered.

Brylee looked at me and rolled her eyes. "Look, Sebastian was always threatening to quit the circus. Wednesday night, I heard him and Monte arguing. I assumed it was because Sebastian threatened to quit again. I don't know."

"Monte is a good man," Tika said. "He would never kill Sebastian."

"And Sebastian got caught with Grigor's Warhammer," Brylee added. "I hate to say it, but maybe Grigor finally took matters into his own hands and killed Sebastian. Have you spoken to him?"

"Not yet," I said. "He's next on my list."

"Brylee has a lot of motive to kill Sebastian," Needles said. *"From his not acknowledging her as his daughter, to not helping with medical bills. She's got a lot of anger inside her."*

"Thank you for your time," I said. "We'll leave you to get back to your visit. I know you don't have much time until your next show, Brylee."

Zoie and I strolled out of the makeshift room and stepped into the main area of the tent.

"I need to use the restroom real quick," I said. "I'll meet you guys out front."

There was a flashing RESTROOM sign not far from where I stood near the back of the tent. Heading that way, I stepped outside into a small courtyard where employee outhouses sat. After doing my business, I stepped back inside the tent and made my way toward the front. I was almost to the entrance when I heard the pixie from earlier, Vaida, talking behind one of the curtains.

"I have something for Ariella," the pixie said. "I don't know how much longer this will hold it off, Brylee. It may be time she tells the truth."

"I understand," Brylee said. "But I need to deal with Mom's situation before I can think about Ariella."

When I heard the curtain being drawn, I hurried out of the tent before they could catch me eavesdropping.

13

"Let's go grab a late lunch," I said as I walked out of the infirmary.

"*Late lunch?*" Needles grumbled. *"It's practically dinner time, Princess!"*

I rolled my eyes and glanced at my watch. "It's two o'clock, Needles."

Zoie laughed. "While you were inside, Shayla, he was trying to talk me into snagging him some salty popcorn."

"Tattletale," Needles grumbled.

I pointed to a stall in the distance. "It looks like they have jumbo turkey legs. Who's up for that?"

Zoie and Needles both raised a hand and a paw in the air.

After standing in line for a few minutes, I handed a turkey leg to Zoie and Needles, and then grabbed mine. I'd always heard the jumbo turkey leg was probably the worst thing you could buy at a fair because who knew if the meat was totally done or not... but I was willing to take my chances.

"Now, this is the life," Needles said, his wings glowing

purple and green as he struggled to hold on to the massive meat stick that was bigger than him.

As we sat apart from the crowds and munched on smoked turkey meat, I filled them in on what I'd overheard as I was exiting the infirmary.

"What do you think it means?" Zoie mused. "Do you think when Ariella almost fell today that it was more than the distraction she claimed?"

I nodded. "I'm beginning to think so. Didn't you notice how she used magic to climb the silks? Why would she need to do that unless she was injured?"

"Maybe she was just saving her strength until her main performance," Needles suggested before taking a huge bite out of his turkey leg.

I shook my head. "I don't know. It seems like we're missing something there."

"Can I confess something?" Zoie asked.

I finished my turkey leg and tossed it in the trash bin. "Of course. Always."

"I really don't want the killer to be Brylee. Her mom doesn't look good, Shayla. What if she dies in the next couple days? Brylee kills her dad because he refused to help pay for medicine to keep her mom alive, and then her mom dies right after that? She spends her life in a PADA cell? It's just...depressing."

I nodded. "I understand, Zoie. I always tried to prepare you for the emotional aspect of this job, and I know your dad did as well, but sometimes life isn't fair. I think it's safe to say none of us here wants to see Brylee be the killer."

"Princess Shayla is correct," Needles said, his wings glowing gray and black. *"Brylee has obviously had a tough upbringing. She has a mother who loved her and yet is dying,*

and a father who rejected her. And she had to see him every day. That had to be difficult."

Zoie tossed her turkey leg in the same trash receptacle and blew out a breath. "I miss my mom, and I'm angry at the way she abandoned me and my dad, but I'm so grateful for the love Dad always showed me." She squared her shoulders. "But if Brylee *is* our killer, then we have to do our job and arrest her."

I nodded. "We do. Now, let's go see Grigor Stonefist. Find out what he has to tell us."

***

We had to wait ten minutes outside Grigor's tent when we arrived because he was in the middle of a performance.

In the distance, I saw GiGi and her gaggle of friends head into Madame Seraphina's fortune-telling tent. I made a mental note to ask GiGi what she'd said to them. If it was anything like what she'd said to me about Needles, GiGi would have a lot to say on that matter.

When Grigor's tent finally emptied out, Zoie, Needles, and I headed inside. He was moving massive amounts of weights off the small platform. He must have heard us because he looked up and grimaced.

"I know why you're here," he grumbled deep in his throat.

"So, you've heard about Sebastian Blackwood?" I asked.

The massive troll nodded his head. "Yes, I have. I've also heard you two are real PADA detectives."

Zoie planted her hands on her hips. "So you understand why we have to ask you some questions?"

"I do."

She nodded. "Good. Can you tell me where you were from 8:30 to 9:30 this morning?"

"That's about the time I got to my tent. It might have been a little after 8:30, but thereabouts. I stayed inside until it was time for the mandatory meeting."

"Were you alone the entire time?" I asked.

A muscle jumped in Grigor's jaw, then he nodded once. "Yes. Just me and my weights." He smiled wickedly. "And my Warhammer."

I narrowed my eyes at Grigor. "Yes, the Warhammer—the motive you have for killing Sebastian."

Grigor lifted his hands in an outward shrug. "Yes, I can see why you might say that." He folded his arms across his chest. "I may have an alibi, but you won't like it, and I'm sure you'd say it was questionable, which is why I didn't even mention it."

I arched a brow. "Care to enlighten us?"

"My son, Manny, stopped by a little before 9:00. He works down at the flying teacups." He smiled a genuine smile. "The ones in kiddieland. My son has a soft spot for the young ones. Monte offered to move him to the adult flying teacups, but he wouldn't have it. Says he enjoys the squeals and screams of the wee ones." He chuckled. "While true, I think he's hoping to prove to the girl he has his eye on that he would make a good father, if you want my opinion."

"I can understand why you would hesitate to tell us about your son," I said. "It's an alibi we'll check out. Thank you. Anyone you can think of who might want to harm Sebastian?"

Grigor leveled his gaze at me, his eyebrows dropping low over his eyes. "I keep to myself."

"So that's a no?" Needles mused. *"Or he knows but isn't willing to say?"*

I didn't think we'd be able to make Grigor talk if he didn't want to, so I simply thanked him again and headed for the tent flap.

"What do you think of his alibi?" Needles asked when we stepped outside.

I shrugged. "He's right about it being suspect, but we'll give it the weight we think it deserves after we speak to his son."

Zoie pointed toward the sky. "Look. Dad's coming in."

14

Alex landed with a soft thud directly in front of Zoie and me. He retracted his wings and shifted back to human form before leaning over and kissing my cheek, then doing the same to Zoie.

"What? No kiss for me?" Needles joked.

Alex chuckled. "Do I need to give you a kiss on the cheek, Needles?"

Needles put one paw to his back. *"Try it, Gargoyle, and those lips will be sliced and diced."*

"Where are you on the investigation?" Alex asked.

I sighed. "We've pretty much talked to everyone on my list of suspects. I'm going to text Grant my list so he can get started on backgrounds for me."

Alex nodded. "Do that now. I told him to go ahead and knock off a little early so he, Serena, and the twins can get to the circus before the dinner crowd arrives."

"I'll do it," Zoie volunteered.

As she texted the list to Grant, Alex surveyed the area. "The circus closes at seven, so that should give them a couple hours of fun."

"I'm not sure the circus is ready for those were-witch twins," Needles said.

"All done," Zoie announced, slipping her cell phone back inside her pocket.

"So where are you headed now?" Alex asked.

"I want to go search Sebastian's personal tent down at the encampment," I said.

"And why is that?" Alex asked as we all turned and headed in that general direction.

"I'm curious if what Brylee said about the thefts are true," I said, filling Alex in on what I'd seen and heard from Brylee.

Willow, Zephyr, Aurora, and Blaze must have been inside The Big Top because they were nowhere to be seen when we passed by their area.

A few minutes later, we stopped in front of Sebastian's tent. Taking down my ward was no problem, but breaking through Sebastian's proved to be a little more difficult. But soon, I was able to flip the flap open, and we all went inside.

"If I didn't know better," I said, "I would call Sebastian a minimalist. This pretty much looks like the inside of his performance tent. Nothing personal, except for these photographs of him with his puppets."

"That's a little strange," Alex said.

"You should have seen the puppets in real life," Needles said. *"Freaked even me out."*

Because there was really nothing inside the tent, it didn't take but a few seconds to go through everything.

When we had completed our task, I stood with my hands on my hips and surveyed the room. "Some of the circus people we spoke to today thought Sebastian was using his puppets to steal, but there's no evidence here Sebastian was a thief."

"Except for yesterday, when you found Grigor's Warhammer," Zoie pointed out. "He did supposedly steal that and tried to hide it in one of the puppet cases."

I grimaced and shook my head. "I don't know. That feels more like a plant. Especially after we've looked through and searched everything in his tent. Why would that object be the only evidence that pointed to the fact Sebastian stole something?"

"And if he *did* steal things," Alex said, "where are they now? We didn't find anything in his tent."

I nodded. "And if Finn had come across any stolen items in the cases, she'd have texted me and told me by now."

"So, what are you thinking?" Zoie asked.

"I'm beginning to wonder if the rumors of Sebastian using his puppets to lift stolen items are just a ruse to throw us off track."

* * *

"Shayla!" Serena called, waving excitedly as she weaved between the throng of Enchanted Island citizens.

Grant walked beside her, carrying one of the twins while the other wriggled in Serena's arms. I heard Cayden's and Brooke's high-pitched squeals and giggles before Grant and Serena finally stopped in front of us.

"You already look exhausted," I joked.

"You have *no* idea," Serena said. "They aren't even one yet, and I *swear* they're excited to be here."

I laughed at the glint of mischief in the twins' eyes. They were way too clever already. Between their strong witch powers and their penchant for shifting into their werewolf forms...poor Grant and Serena were constantly on their toes.

I glanced behind them. "Where's Zac, Tamara, and Jayden?"

"They're right behind us," Serena said as she gladly gave Brooke to Alex.

Sure enough, the newly married family came bounding over—Tamara looking happy despite wrangling a rambunctious toddler, who was clearly excited and ready to explore the circus. Not even a month had passed since Tamara had adopted Jayden, and Zac and Tamara had gotten married.

"We're just stopping by to say hi," Zac said. "Jayden is already begging us to ride the flying teacups."

Tamara groaned. "Thankfully, she has to ride the kiddie rides. Although she's told us in no uncertain terms exactly what she thinks of that."

"Dumb," Jayden pouted as she crossed her chubby little arms over her chest. "Wanna ride big people rides."

"I know you do, honey," Zac soothed. "Maybe in a couple years."

Jayden pursed her lips and stared at the twins. "Dumb."

And I *swear*...the twins both nodded their heads.

"You all saw that, right?" Needles demanded, his wings glowing red and orange. *"Wait until I tell Black Forest King. He tells me not to worry, but I swear these three will sink this island before they reach puberty!"*

Luckily, Tamara and Zac couldn't understand Needles...but it didn't keep the rest of us from chuckling at Needles' tirade. It was a well-known fact Needles was both in awe of the magical talents the youngers showed...and a little bit afraid.

"We better head out," Tamara said. "Have fun, you guys."

"Same to you!" we all called out as we waved goodbye.

"Here comes your mom," Alex said, wrapping his baby-free arm around my waist.

I reached up and tickled Brooke's cheek while we all waited for Mom to reach us.

"Quite a crowd," Mom said, leaning over to kiss my cheek before doing the same to Brooke. "How's my favorite baby girl?" She turned to Cayden, who was practically leaping out of Grant's arm. "And my favorite baby boy?" She snagged Cayden to her and kissed his cheek as well.

"Ornery," Serena and Grant said simultaneously…causing us all to laugh.

"Let's go to the face-painting booth," Zoie said. "I've been waiting all day to paint these adorable babies' cheeks!"

The twins clapped and babbled, which we took to mean it was a good idea to them as well. As we headed toward the face-painting booth, I kept an eye out for GiGi, Byron, Gertrude, and Hagatha. If they were still here, they'd never forgive us if we didn't stop by and say hi with the twins.

15

"Where's GiGi?" I asked Mom as we all started walking toward the face-painting booth.

"She and Byron are in the Princess Lolly taking a nap," Mom said.

I laughed. "*What? Are you serious?*"

"Yep," Mom said.

"How are they *both* squeezing into that death ride?" I demanded.

Mom shrugged. "You know GiGi. She was determined to stay until we all got here. So if it means she and Byron fold themselves like an accordion to rest, then they'll do it."

The Princess Lolly was a tiny contraption of a car that was barely street legal. It topped out at fifty miles-per-hour and was designed to look like it had just jumped out of the classic kids' game *Candyland*. It even had giant lollipops welded on the top of the roof.

"I just texted her," Mom said. "They should meet up with us shortly."

There was a long line for the face-painting booth, so Alex and Grant offered to get us drinks while we waited. Taking Brooke from Alex, I pointed to the chart displaying everything from enchanted animals to mystical designs.

"Which one do you want?" I asked Brooke as Serena, Cayden, Zoie, and Mom stood next to me.

"Don't show them the dragon!" Needles chided from my shoulder.

The twins immediately started babbling and pointing to the picture of the flying dragon.

I couldn't help the grin that spread across my face. "Have you figured out what you're gonna do for their one-year birthdays next month?"

Serena groaned. "I think so. I'm still waiting to hear back on a couple things, though. I wish I knew a good party planner."

I laughed. "You bake for parties all the time."

Serena rolled her eyes. "It's not the same. There's a lot of pressure here."

I frowned and raised one hand. "For the twins' first birthday? They aren't even gonna remember it, Serena."

"You have *no* idea of the social pressures," she insisted.

I was about to press for more information when the line moved and we were next. As Serena and I sat in the vacant chairs holding the babies on our laps, Zoie took pictures on her phone while Needles hovered near her shoulder, turning somersaults in the air. Alex and Grant arrived with drinks and helped to keep the twins entertained while the artists worked their magic as quickly as they could.

When the face-painting was done, the twins were absolutely glowing. I leaned in closer, admiring the realistic detail of work on Brooke's chubby cheek. "That dragon looks very lifelike."

Needles groaned. *"Don't say that, Princess!"*

Before I could get up from my chair…a burst of flames shot out from the side of Brooke's face, causing me to let out a yelp, and everyone in line to scream.

"Is that supposed to happen?" Serena demanded.

The artist paled as she shook her head emphatically. "No. The dragon is just supposed to flap his wings."

I grinned over at Brooke. "You little stinker. Are you doing that?"

Brooke looked over at her brother and babbled something. As Serena stood with Cayden, he let out a squeal and the crowd screamed again as *his* dragon leaped from his right cheek, shot out a stream of fire, then flew to the other side of his face to rest on his left cheek.

"That's some high-level magic," Zoie whispered.

My mom met my eyes and gave a small nod. Even she was impressed with the twins' magical abilities. And even though we teased Needles about his worry…I think there was a small part in all of us that was scared he might just be a little right when it came to what these two would do before they reached their teenage years.

"Why don't Alex, Grant, and I take these adorable babies over to the kiddie section," Mom suggested. "You girls take a breather and meet up with us in a bit."

Zoie glanced at her watch when we were baby-free and husband-free. "Harlow is supposed to be here by now."

"Alone or with her new boyfriend?" Serena demanded as we started strolling the grounds.

Zoie grinned. "With her beau."

"I can't wait to meet him," I said.

Needles leaped from my shoulder and whipped out a quill. *"He better be a good one, or I'll run him through with one of my quills."*

"Hey," I whispered, slowing my pace. "Look over at Monte's tent, but don't be obvious."

"Who's Monte?" Serena hissed.

I smiled. "Just look over where the tent is that says OFFICE."

"That's Nathaniel Nyx," Zoie said. "I wonder what they're talking about."

The two men had their heads together and were talking quickly. We couldn't hear what they were saying, but whatever it was they were discussing, it was getting animated.

"Who feels like doing an impromptu stakeout?" I grinned.

* * *

"How exactly are we going to do a stakeout?" Zoie whispered as she, Serena, Needles, and I ducked behind a tent selling circus memorabilia just a few feet from Nathanial and Monte.

I glanced at Needles and tried to hide my smile as an idea came to me.

"I don't like that look, Princess," Needles grumbled as he fluttered from my shoulder. *"What am I gonna have to do?"*

"We're gonna glamor you," I said.

Serena and Zoie whisper-squealed as they silently clapped their hands.

"What should we glamor him as?" Zoie demanded, barely able to contain her excitement.

"Nothing that will bring attention to us." I bit my lip and narrowed my eyes, contemplating Needles. "I'll do a simple glamor of an owl. Think you can pull that off, Needles?"

Needles' wings glowed red and black. *"Hoot...hoot."*

I let out a soft laugh at his deadpanned imitation. "How about we just go in silent? You can leave out the hoots."

I whispered the spell that transformed my flying and talking porcupine into a majestic owl—fluffy, with huge dark eyes. In place of his sharp quills were now soft feathers.

"I demand an extra-salty pretzel before we leave here tonight," Needles grumbled.

I smiled. "Deal. Now, go listen in and see what they're saying."

Needles flew away and perched on the roof of Monte's tent. It didn't exactly look natural, but as long as no one pointed him out, I figured we were okay.

Needles turned his massive owl-like head, blinked, and let out a loud, *"Hoot, hoot,"* in the same monotoned way he'd done just minutes before.

Zoie giggled. "He just had to get the last word."

"Here he comes," Serena hissed.

The three of us pressed our backs against the tent we were peeking out from behind and waited until Needles hovered in front of us.

"I will tell you what they said when you make me my beautiful former self," he said.

Moving my hand in the air, I took away Needles' glamor. "Now, dish."

"From what I could understand, they're very worried."

I frowned. "Worried about what?"

Needles shrugged and landed on my shoulder. *"I don't know. Nathaniel was asking Monte if he got a look inside before the police came."*

Zoie frowned. "Look inside what? Sebastian's personal tent? Or his performance tent?"

"I do not know, Miss Zoie. That is all they were talking about. Nathaniel asked Monte twice if Monte got a look inside before the police came."

"And what did Monte say?" I asked.

"He said he did not get a look inside before the police came."

The three of us stood there and pondered what Needles had just told us. I was about to suggest we go find Mom, the boys, and the twins when Zoie pointed off in the distance. "Looks like Dad, Serenity, and Grant found Harlow and Dominic."

"And here comes GiGi and Byron as well," I said. "This is shaping up to be a fun night."

16

"We finally get to meet the new guy," I gushed. "This should be fun. What did you say his name was again?"

"Dominic." Pressing her lips together and trying not to smile, Zoie shook her finger at me. "And do *not* embarrass Harlow." Zoie grinned. "She may hex you."

Needles leaped from my shoulder and did a somersault, his wings glowing purple and green. *"I can't wait!"*

"I take it you've met him?" Serena mused.

Zoie bit her lip and nodded…again, I got the impression she was trying not to laugh. "Many times."

"What?" I demanded. "Dish!"

Zoie giggled. "You'll see. I adore him. I think he's fabulous."

The first things I noticed about Dominic were his enthusiastic smile and laughing hazel eyes. Mainly because it was a complete contrast to Harlow's serious face. His brown hair was windblown and slightly messy, and he ran his hands through it as though to tame it when he came to a stop in front of us. He was dressed in red pants, a purple shirt, and yellow Converse. It looked like a bag of Skittles had exploded on him. It was a complete contrast to Harlow's black mini-dress, black leggings, black sandals, and blonde braids. At least she was wearing her purple lipstick.

I caught Alex's grin and figured he must have already been introduced to Dominic.

"Wait for me!" GiGi huffed as she and Byron hurried over to us. "I want to meet the new guy too."

Even with Alex, Grant, Serena, Mom, GiGi, Byron, and me all clamoring to meet Dominic...he didn't look the least bit uncomfortable. In fact, he looked like he was having a great time.

"I'm Dominic Chase." He stuck out his hand and shook all of ours. "Lovely to meet you all. I've already had the pleasure of meeting Alex, Grant, and Serenity just now. I'm glad to finally put a face with the names."

Brooke and Cayden babbled and waved, and I softened a little when Dominic grinned and blew a kiss to both babies.

"So you're the new beau, huh?" GiGi demanded. She was bending from side to side as though checking him out completely. "Not bad. Not bad." She grinned. "For a vampire."

Dominic threw back his head and laughed. "Thank you! And you must be GiGi. I've heard all about you."

GiGi nodded and crossed her arms over her chest. "No surprise. I'm a legend around these parts."

I snorted. "In your own mind."

"Watch it," GiGi snapped as she pointed a finger at me. "I can still make you get zits with one zap."

"Watch it yourself, Dragon Lady," Needles warned.

"Mom," my mother chided. "Behave yourself."

"I come from a large family," Dominic said. "I'm used to the teasing."

GiGi pursed her lips together. "Your family lives on Enchanted Island?"

Dominic shook his head. "No. They live in Haunted Bay. It's a paranormal town outside Savannah, Georgia."

"So you're a move in," GiGi said. "When did that happen, and why? Are you running from the law?"

"Geez, GiGi," I said. "If the guy is gonna get interrogated, it'll be by Alex, Grant, or me."

Dominic held up his hands and grinned. "It's cool. Like I said, I have my own GiGi back in Haunted Bay."

"She must be stunning and smart," GiGi deadpanned.

"Absolutely," Dominic said.

We quickly went around the circle and gave him our names. When I introduced Needles, Dominic grinned and became extra enthusiastic. "A talking and flying porcupine. That's wonderful! It must be an absolute thrill to be his friend. His colors are gorgeous."

"I like him," Needles said. *"He can stay alive another day."*

"So what do you do?" I asked, trying to steer the conversation back to Dominic.

I wasn't sure, but I swear I heard Harlow groan. I glanced at her questioningly…but she stared me down, not even cracking a smile.

"I moved here about six months ago," Dominic said. "I'd just turned twenty-five, and I had a sort of mid-life crisis."

Alex laughed. "At twenty-five?"

Dominic grinned. "Okay, a mid-twenties crisis. Anyway, I realized if I continued down the path I was going, I'd end up like the rest of my family. Living in the same small town, not really achieving my goals, and just working a job." He threw up his hands. "So I started looking on the supernatural internet for the top five supernatural towns to live in, and Enchanted Island came up. And I thought how cool is that! It's not a town, but an entire island. I found a small place to rent for my business, was thrilled when it came with an upstairs apartment, and the rest is history. Been here about six months and can't wait to get my business up and running."

"And what exactly is it you do?" I asked.

"Same thing I did back in Haunted Bay," Dominic said. "Only I hope it can really take off here on an island."

"And what is this job?" Alex pushed.

Dominic whipped out a handful of business cards so quickly, I almost thought he'd used magic. "I sort of have two jobs right now since my main job hasn't exactly taken off yet."

Zoie giggled, and Harlow shot her a death glare. I almost felt sorry for Zoie, but she looked totally unfazed as Zoie grinned up at Dominic. "Dominic has the *best* jobs."

"To offset the slow time right now," Dominic said, "I invested the last of my savings into the ice cream truck Buford Mapleton was selling. As of five days ago, I'm now the ice cream truck guy!"

Serena gasped and clapped her hands together. "That's *you* I've seen driving up and down the streets this last week?"

Cayden and Brooke suddenly righted themselves off Alex's and Grant's shoulders, where they'd been slowly falling asleep. "Cream! Cream!"

Serena laughed. "The twins love ice cream."

"He sells ice cream from a truck?" Needles mused. *"Is that really a thing? Does he sell salty ice cream?"*

"Have you gone on an ice cream truck ride, Harlow?" GiGi asked with laughter in her eyes.

Dominic laughed and pulled Harlow close to his side. "Not

yet. She's still a little hesitant." He smiled down at her. "But I'll wear her down. Pretty soon, she'll be handing out ice cream by my side and loving every minute of it."

I couldn't help the bark of laughter that burst out of me. I tried to cover it with a cough…but I wasn't fooling anyone. Least of all Harlow.

"And your other job?" GiGi demanded.

I could tell she was just as amused at the thought of Harlow's new guy selling ice cream out of a truck and thinking Harlow would someday be right by his side handing out ice cream to little kids right along with him, smiling and singing.

"I'm an event planner," Dominic said, his chest puffing just a little. "That's the job I feel called to the most. I *love* celebrating with people during their happiest of times."

"Has he met *Harlow?"* Needles whispered in my ear.

Serena and Zoie giggled, while Harlow shot Needles more death daggers.

"Well, now," GiGi said, "I can see why you and Harlow make such a great couple."

Dominic glanced down at Harlow, still close by his side, and smiled as he nodded. "I think so too."

It was clear the guy was gaga over Harlow.

"I agree," Mom said.

I caught Alex's eyes, and he grinned. I was sure he'd have a lot to say on the ride home.

Serena gasped and clutched at Dominic's arm. "Oh, my goddess. I just thought of something! Please tell me you have an opening in your schedule?"

"What are you looking to do?" Dominic asked.

Grant laughed. "Yes, please tell us you have time. Serena is going out of her mind trying to plan this party."

"I love a good party!" Dominic said to Serena. "Who's it for? You? Your husband?"

"The twins!" Serena exclaimed. "They're turning one."

Dominic's face lit up with so much joy, I thought he was going to burst and shoot out confetti from his body! He clapped his hands in glee. "A baby birthday party! And for *twins!* Oh, I'd *love* to get together and talk ideas."

Tears filled Serena's eyes. "I'd truly appreciate any help I could get. I thought I could handle it on my own, but I was wrong."

Dominic nodded sagely. "It's true. Most people think it's easy to throw something together, and then when they get near the day, they start to panic."

"So you can help?" Serena asked.

"Absolutely," Dominic said.

"Well," Harlow said, reaching down and clasping Dominic's hand. "Now that that's done, Dom, Zoie, and I are out. I suddenly feel the need to walk through a clown house and be tortured until I scream and beg for mercy."

I thought the twins might pipe up with more shouts of ice cream…but they were already fast asleep. We waved goodbye to Zoie, Harlow, and Dominic…then all started talking at once.

"I like him," Mom said.

"You think he's always that chipper and happy?" GiGi asked.

"How did they meet again?" Grant asked.

"They met at the grocery store," I said. "They both reached for the last bag of blood puffs, or something like that."

Alex nodded. "It should be an interesting courtship."

I snickered. "I don't think they call them courtships anymore."

Alex frowned and carefully shifted Cayden in his arms. "They don't?"

I was about to respond when I saw Ariella Moonshadow hurrying toward her performance tent. Because I wanted to know what potion the pixie's were making for her on the sly, I quickly excused myself and promised to be right back.

"Ariella," I called, rushing over to her.

"I'm late," Ariella said. "I can't talk now."

"We can walk and talk," I said.

Ariella scowled. "Fine."

"I want to talk about the potion the pixies are making you," I said. "You know, the one no one is supposed to know about."

Ariella stopped walking and whirled to face me, her eyes wide with fear. "How do you know?"

I shrugged. "I just do. And before you think someone told me, they didn't. I just happened to find out."

Tears filled her eyes as she started speed walking again. "Please don't tell Monte. Not yet."

"Why are you taking it?" I asked.

We'd finally reached her tent, but instead of going inside, Ariella steered me to the side. "I have amyotrophic lateral sclerosis. It's found in both humans and supernaturals. Basically, it's a disease that affects the motor neurons in the brain, spinal cord, and brainstem. It causes muscle loss and atrophy." A tear slipped down her cheek and she brushed it away. "The loss of strength in my arms is just the start."

"Did Sebastian know?" I asked. "I can't imagine it was something you could keep from him if you dated all that time."

Another tear trailed down her cheek, and this time, she let it fall to the ground. "He knew. When I begged him not to tell anyone, and let me tell Monte in my own time, he said he'd think about it." Her words caught on a sob. "At that moment, I totally understood what Brylee meant when she talked about hating

Sebastian. He was cold and calloused, and he didn't care about anyone other than himself and those damn puppets." She sucked in a breath and wiped her face. "Now, if you'll excuse me, the show must go on."

17

"Grant just texted and said he has bakery items for us," I said the minute Zoie hopped inside my Bronco around 9:30 the next morning. "So we can bypass Bakery & Brew and go straight to the station."

"Perfect." Zoie buckled herself up then peeked around the seat. "Morning, Needles."

"Good morning, Miss Zoie. Lovely day to solve a murder and eat a pretzel, wouldn't you say?"

Zoie laughed and turned back around in her seat. "I would say you're exactly right."

I pulled up to the front of the station and shut off the Bronco. Most times, I just pulled against the curb and parked because it was convenient and easy. There was a parking lot out back, but I preferred going in the front.

The minute I pulled the door open, Needles headed up the stairs to the sheriff's office, while Zoie and I headed downstairs where the labs were—medical, forensics, and IT. But first, I had to get past the octogenarian dragon lady, Pearl Earthly-Caraway.

"Miss Zoie," Pearl said as she looked up from the crossword she was currently working on. "I heard you had your first assignment as a detective with PADA. Congratulations!"

"Thanks, Mrs. Earthly-Caraway. Harlow and Needles helped a lot. I couldn't have done it without them."

Pearl ran her eyes up and down my form. "Yes, we like that Harlow girl."

I bit back a smile. What Pearl was saying without having to come out and say it was that she liked Harlow... not so much me.

"Ooh, good one, Pearl," I said dryly. "Nice burn."

Pearl grinned. "What? I didn't say anything." She glanced down at her crossword and circled something on the paper. "Well, go on, you two. Don't keep them waiting. Everyone's got jobs around here."

"Yes, ma'am," Zoie and I said simultaneously.

We hurried down the hall and stopped at the first door on the right. Knocking once, I pushed open the door and stepped inside.

Finn and Harlow were standing in front of a massive computer screen, pointing at something, while Doc was on the opposite side of the room, standing next to Sebastian Blackwood's dead body.

"Morning," I said. "Harlow, did you have fun at the circus last night?"

Finn glanced questioningly at Harlow. "You didn't tell me you went to the circus. What'd you think?"

I laughed at the daggers Harlow shot me. "You didn't tell them about you and your guy doing the circus thing?"

Finn gasped. "What? What's this about a new guy? Why didn't you tell me?"

Harlow narrowed her eyes at me before turning back to Finn. "Because we're at work."

"We like him," I said.

"Who is this young man?" Doc asked as he strolled over to where we stood.

"You guys don't know him," Harlow grumbled. "He's new to the island."

"And a party planner!" I added joyfully. "And, until his business gets up and running, he's also the ice cream truck driver."

Finn clasped her hands to her chest. "Wait, you mean that cute vampire I've seen cruising around? Oh, he's a doll."

I laughed. "Don't let Jordan hear you say that. He might get jealous."

Finn waved her hand dismissively in the air. "Jordan never gets jealous." She continued to study Harlow, like she was a slide under one of her fancy microscopes. "So, you're going for an opposites-attract kind of thing? Is that it?"

"How about I just like him?" Harlow mused. "He makes me laugh... sometimes."

Doc chuckled and waved us over to the body. "Come on, come on. Let me tell you what I found."

We strolled behind him as he sidled up to the table and shifted the sheet a little lower.

"Sebastian Blackwood. Age, fifty-three. Fairy. Overall, good health at the time of death. No legal, illegal, or supernatural drugs found in his body." He pointed to the marks around his neck. "Cause of death is asphyxiation. You can see where he was strangled."

"Harlow and I examined the puppet strings," Finn said. "They had traces of magic on them, but it's unclear whether they were enchanted just to do the murder or if they had already been enchanted."

I nodded. "It's common knowledge Sebastian used magic to enchant his strings."

"We also examined the water found on the ground in Sebastian's tent," Harlow said. "It came back as saltwater."

Zoie looked at me. "So, does that mean the water was from Nathaniel Nyx's tank?"

"Possibly," I said. "I want to double-check and make sure there was nobody in his tent earlier that morning."

Zoie furrowed her brow and frowned. "But couldn't someone have gotten the water the day before and planted it?"

I nodded. "Yes, that's what makes it hard. What about the puppets? Did you find anything there?"

Finn and Harlow nodded and fist-bumped each other.

"Oh, yeah," Finn said. "We found a lot."

She motioned for us to follow her out of the room and down the hallway until we came to a door on the right. Opening it, we stepped inside.

"Yep, still creepy," Zoie said.

The five dolls stood at attention in the room, strings straight up in the air on three of them, strings down on the other two.

"Come check this out," Finn said.

We hurried over to where the schoolmarm puppet was. Lifting the doll's hair, she pushed a lever. I heard a small click but didn't see anything different about the puppet. Grinning, Finn unzipped the back of the puppet's dress, revealing an open compartment.

"You've got to be kidding," I said, glancing down into the hollowed-out space.

Inside were two rings, a watch, a money clip full of bills, and a diamond earring.

"That's not all," Harlow said. "We found a secret compartment in the other puppets as well."

Zoie crossed her arms over her chest and nodded. "I'd say

this could be what Nathaniel and Monte were talking about last night, when Nathaniel asked Monte if he was able to get a look inside. He wasn't talking about the tents. He was talking about the puppets."

"I'd have to agree," I said.

18

"Good morning, you two," Opal Earthly-Caraway said as Zoie and I strolled inside the sheriff's station a few minutes later.

A complete contrast to her dour twin sister downstairs, Opal was always pleasant and greeted you with a smile on her face.

"Morning, Opal," Zoie and I said simultaneously.

Alex and Grant were across the room near the windows. One of Serena's bakery boxes was on the table, lid open. Next to it was Needles, hovering in the air, chowing down on a caramel-dipped pretzel rod.

"*All I'm saying,*" Needles said as Zoie and I strolled over to where Alex and Grant sat, "*is why not have a candy machine put in that's only filled with bags of pretzels? This way, you can always have them on hand. I only found two small bags in the lounge.*" He held up the half-eaten rod in his paw, his wings glowing purple and blue. "*Thankfully, Serena took pity on me and packed me this lovely caramel-dipped delight.*" He turned to me, his wings fluttering double-time. *"Help a porcupine out, Princess. Don't you think my idea is brilliant?"*

"No, it's not," Alex said before I could say a word.

"No one asked you, Gargoyle," Needles snapped.

"You were *literally* just trying to convince me to put in a vending machine," Alex said dryly.

Grant chuckled. "Help yourself to some goodies. Coffee should be done brewing by now."

I glanced over and saw the full pot of black coffee. Waving my hand in the air, I used my magic to transfer over the pot, four cups, and a container holding sugar and powdered creamer. While Zoie and I picked out our goodies—a cinnamon roll for her, and a cranberry-orange muffin for me—I filled the guys in on what we'd learned downstairs, including the hidden compartments on the puppets.

"That slimy snake," Needles said.

"Let's get started then." Grant opened the file on his desk and picked up the page on top. "First up is Monte Vex. Seventy-five-year-old-witch. Widow, no children. Owns Monte's Magical Circus. He has a criminal record for trespassing, performing without proper supernatural permits, and possession of stolen goods—namely, a four-foot clown head and two cotton candy machines. His financials are somewhat precarious. The circus just barely breaks even each year. I did notice he's been spending a lot of money lately on medicinal potions."

I nodded. "We figured as much."

"Motive?" Alex asked.

I sat back in my chair. "It's no secret Monte has been struggling to keep the circus afloat financially and is under immense pressure because of it. The victim, Sebastian Blackwood, recently threatened to leave the circus and take his talents elsewhere, which would have been a massive blow to both the circus's reputation and its finances."

"More than one person we spoke to," Zoie added, "told us without Sebastian and his act, the circus would be in financial trouble. Sebastian and his puppets were the headliner, and he made sure everyone knew it."

"But why kill his lead act?" Grant asked.

"I got the impression Monte was tired of Sebastian's constant threats," I said. "I do know he has Nathaniel Nyx chomping away to take over the head position. Could be Monte had enough of the threats and just decided to make room for a different act."

Alex took a sip of his coffee. "Alibi?"

"Monte claimed he was in his office going over the circus' finances during the time of death window," I said. "He left the office around 9:00 to go to The Big Top and get ready to conduct a mandatory meeting."

"So no one can corroborate his alibi?" Alex asked.

I shook my head. "Not that we know of." I took a sip of my coffee. "Two things to note. Brylee Flare said she overheard Monte and Sebastian arguing on Wednesday night. The other thing is last night, as I just mentioned, Needles went in undercover and found out Monte and Nathaniel Nyx were talking, and Nathaniel asked Monte if he got a look inside before the police arrived. At the time we didn't know what Nathaniel meant, but now that we know about the hidden compartments in the puppets, I think we need to talk with both men again."

"Nathaniel was Sebastian's understudy," Zoie said. "I'm voting he knew about the compartments."

"I agree with Miss Zoie," Needles said.

"We also need to corner Monte today and get a look at Sebastian's will," I said to Zoie. "He's had long enough to produce it."

"Next up," Grant said, "is Ariella Moonshadow or Linda

Stark." He looked up and grinned. "Most of the names are stage names or performance names."

I nodded. "Figured as much."

Grant took a bite of his cinnamon roll before continuing. "Ariella Moonshadow. Age, forty-four. Witch. Divorced, no children. She's an aerialist and contortionist for Monte's Magical Circus. She does have a criminal record, all dating back to the age of eighteen."

"Probably why she joined the paranormal circus," Alex said. "Make a fresh start."

Grant nodded. "Probably. So a criminal record of low-level hexing and shoplifting. Her financials don't really show any red flags. She makes just enough money to get by and keeps her debt down."

"And her motive to want Sebastian Blackwood dead?" Alex mused.

Zoie's eye lit up. "It's a big one, but sort of sad. Ariella and Sebastian dated for a while, but he recently broke up with her. That would be bad enough if it stopped there, but Ariella has—what was it again, Shayla?"

"Amyotrophic lateral sclerosis."

"What's that?" Alex asked.

"A disease that causes her muscles to atrophy," I said.

"Shayla, Needles, and I witnessed it firsthand when we were talking with her," Zoie cut in. "She has to use magic just to propel her up the silks. She was up there and almost fell, but told us she was just distracted with everything going on. Shayla later found out she has this debilitating disease, and Sebastian knew and threatened to tell Monte."

I nodded. "Ariella admitted she wasn't ready to tell Monte yet because she wasn't ready to retire."

Grant took a bite of his cinnamon roll and nodded. "So

Ariella may have decided to take out the threat to her livelihood."

"Yep," Zoie said, finishing off her roll.

"Alibi?" Alex asked.

"Ariella claims to have been in her tent checking the silks," Zoie said. "She met up with Brylee Flare around 9:15, and they walked over to The Big Top together."

"I have a working theory when it comes to Ariella," I said.

"Let's hear it," Alex said as he shoved the last of his cinnamon roll in his mouth.

"Ariella told us the last time she spoke to Sebastian was the night before he died—on Thursday evening." I finished off my muffin and took a sip of coffee to wash it down. "She tried to tell him she didn't believe he'd stolen Grigor's Warhammer. What if Ariella was the one who stole the Warhammer, then put it in Sebastian's tent so he'd take the fall? She hoped to get him fired, thereby keeping her secret hidden for a while longer. When that didn't work, and Sebastian wasn't fired, she decided to kill him."

Alex nodded. "I can see that. Who's next?"

"Brylee Flare," Grant said. "Age, twenty-five. Half elemental witch, half fairy. Single, no children. She has a fire act in Monte's Magical Circus. No criminal record. From the looks of her financials, she worked more as a backup act until two years ago."

"That's probably when her mom started to get sick," I said.

"Brylee's mom is dying," Zoie said, sorrow etched in her voice.

"She has Infernal Decay." I met Alex's eyes. "It's serious enough she may not live out the week."

Alex winced. "That's unfortunate."

"But that's not the worst," Zoie said. "Brylee's dad is Sebastian Blackwood. According to both Brylee and her mom, Sebastian never acknowledged Brylee as his daughter!" She shook her head. "I mean, can you imagine that? They worked the same job and probably saw each other every day, and Sebastian never admitted Brylee was his daughter."

"Makes for some hard feelings," Grant said.

Alex nodded. "I'd agree."

"Brylee's financials are a mess," Grant said. "She's in debt up to her eyeballs. When I dug deeper, I could see that most of her money goes to medicinal potions, just like Monte Vex."

I nodded. "They both are trying to keep Tika Blaze alive as long as possible."

"Motive?" Alex asked.

I reached over and snagged a cake pop from the box. "There's plenty. Brylee has a father who refuses to acknowledge her, but the final straw is knowing he could financially help keep her mother alive, but refuses. According to Brylee, the potions can keep Tika alive and help prolong her life, but the financial cost is steep. The ingredients are expensive. And she's right. I looked up the ingredients, and each potion that is made probably costs around $500. Tika needs a boost about every three days."

Alex whistled. "That's steep. Especially when you're making a living with the circus. I can't imagine it pays much."

"Brylee falls into the low-income category," Grant said. "And she's heavily in debt."

Zoie sighed and took a sip of her heavily doctored coffee. "I really don't want Brylee to be the killer. It's like she can't catch a break. Mom is dying, and her father never cared about her."

"Still doesn't mean you have the right to kill someone," Alex pointed out.

Zoie nodded. "I know, Dad. But it still sucks."

"It does," I agreed. "I think the biggest nail in the coffin for Brylee came when I spoke to Blaze, the phoenix."

"You spoke to a phoenix?" Grant mused. "That's one for the record books."

I laughed. "She's a beauty. Anyway, Blaze told me she overheard Brylee and Sebastian arguing Wednesday evening when she was out flying. Brylee demanded Sebastian help pay for her mom's medical bills, and Sebastian made a reference to the fact he'd help pay over his dead body."

We all just sat there for a second...taking that in.

"Alibi?" Alex asked.

"Brylee was at the infirmary sitting with her mom at 7:00. She left around 8:45. That leaves a window of at least twenty minutes before she met back up with Ariella for the meeting. When questioned what she did in that twenty-minute time, Brylee couldn't really account for it. She said she might have walked slower than usual. She thinks she did some meditating while thinking about her mom. She then tried to redirect us by stating Monte and Sebastian were always arguing lately. Which really upset Tika. She was quick to defend Monte and say he couldn't be the killer."

"Next up," Grant said, pouring himself more coffee, "we have Nathaniel Nyx. Real name Nathaniel Reed. Age, twenty-nine. Half witch, half merman. Single, no children. He works as an escape artist for Monte's Magical Circus. Like Ariella, his criminal history was when he was nineteen. Shoplifting, possession of stolen items, and possession of a controlled magical substance. The supernatural court gave him three months in jail. Nothing on his record since then. Financials show he joined Monte's Magical Circus at the age of twenty. He has no major debt."

"Motive?" Alex said.

"He was Sebastian's apprentice for about four years when he first got hired on at the circus," I said. "A few years back, the two men broke their partnership when Nathaniel started pushing for more headliner time with the puppets. Monte moved Nathaniel to be the understudy for the escape artist, Luna. When Luna married one of the clowns and had babies, she gave Nathaniel the center stage to be the sole escape artist. It was all on the up and up." I poured another cup of coffee and added a little cream and sugar. "After talking with Nathaniel, it was clear there was no love lost between the two men. And if Nathaniel thought he could be the star headliner for the circus instead of Sebastian, then he'd take that opportunity."

"Alibi?" Alex asked.

"Nathaniel has an understudy—Esta Topaz," I said. "Nathaniel told us he and Esta arrived at the tent a little after 8:30. I can confirm that. I saw him enter his tent around that time as well. He said he and Esta were in the water tank warming up until around 9:00. That's when Esta left to get something she forgot in her tent down at the encampment. She left, leaving Nathaniel alone for fifteen minutes before the mandatory meeting."

"Which brings us to Esta Topaz," Grant said. "Real name is Esta Marley. Age, twenty-eight. Single, no children. Half witch, half mermaid. She, too, works for Monte's Magical Circus. Not a lot on Esta. She joined the circus around age twenty-three. According to PADA, there's no criminal record for Esta. Her financials are like most who work at the circus there—low income, but she lives within her means and doesn't have a lot of debt."

"Motive to kill Sebastian?" Alex asked.

"Not sure," I said honestly.

"She seems eager to have a bigger role," Needles said.

I nodded. "She does. But I'm not sure killing Sebastian would be the way to go about getting a bigger role. As far as we know, she's not a puppeteer. I felt her name needed to be added to our list of possible suspects because for fifteen minutes, she didn't have a solid alibi during Sebastian's time of death. I was thinking more along the lines of her infatuation for Nathaniel caused her to kill for him."

"*She was pretty enamored with Nathaniel,*" Needles agreed.

"Exactly," I said. "Maybe she killed Sebastian, hoping Nathaniel would become the headliner, and thereby giving him what he wants."

"But I didn't get a boyfriend-girlfriend vibe from them," Zoie said. "I mean, I think she'd be okay with it, but Nathaniel didn't talk to her or touch her like she was anything more than his helper."

"Which could support your motive, Shayla," Alex said. "She killed Sebastian more for Nathaniel than for herself, maybe hoping to gain his affection."

I nodded. "Yeah. Something like that. It's still a working theory."

"And her alibi?" Grant asked.

"Is the reason I had to put her down on the list," I said. "She left Nathaniel's tent around 9:00, stating she forgot a garment she'd been working on back at her tent at the encampment. Now, I've timed that to be about five minutes there and back if she jogged. If she stopped and strangled Sebastian in that time, it would be close, but I suppose doable. But it also leaves Nathaniel free for fifteen minutes."

Zoie reached inside the bakery box and snagged a cake pop. "I remember when Esta came into The Big Top for the mandatory meeting, she was panting heavily and carrying the garment."

"Lastly," Grant said, "I have Grigor Stonefist. Age, forty-eight. Troll. Widowed, one adult son who also works at the circus. Wife passed away six years ago. Grigor is the strongman for Monte's Magical Circus. He does have a detailed criminal record from eighteen up to twenty-three…all in supernatural courts. Brawling, disorderly conduct, property damage, smuggling magical goods, unlicensed fighting. He did a couple months here and there in different jails."

"He doesn't mind using his fists when angry," Alex said.

"We are a lot alike in that aspect," Needles said. *"I got paws of fury and quills that will make a person scream."*

Zoie held up a finger. "But Sebastian wasn't beaten…he was strangled."

"Grigor would still be using his hands," Alex countered.

Zoie nodded. "Very true, Dad."

"Grigor's financials are like everyone else's. He gets by, has almost no debt, but not much to his name, either. Not sure what his wife died of, but it must not have required medical or magical treatment."

"Motive?" Grant asked.

"The day before Sebastian was murdered," I said, "Grigor accused Sebastian of stealing his Warhammer. Zoie and I found the Warhammer in Sebastian's tent. Since it couldn't be proven if it was stolen or planted, Monte just gave the Warhammer back to Grigor, but not before Grigor threatened Sebastian and told him to watch his back."

"Alibi?" Alex asked.

"Grigor told us he was in his tent lifting weights to blow off steam before the mandatory meeting," I said. "I personally saw Grigor enter his tent around 8:40. He also told us his son, Manny, came to visit him around 9:00, and the two walked to the meeting together a little while later. We still need to question Manny."

"Even though Grigor can't wield magic," Zoie said, "he is strong enough to strangle and kill someone. We also know the strings Sebastian used were enchanted, so it could be Grigor picked up the magical strings and strangled Sebastian, then left the strings around Sebastian's neck hoping we'd think the killer had magical abilities because the strings were enchanted."

Alex nodded. "Very true."

"Let's talk about the clues left behind at the scene of the crime," I said. "First, we have standing water near the body. According to forensics, the water contained saltwater. I'm pretty sure if we analyze the water in Nathaniel's tank, we'll find traces of saltwater."

"Why would he leave the water behind?" Alex asked.

"In a hurry?" Grant mused.

"Didn't realize he was making that much of a mess?" Zoie supplied.

"Bad luck," Needles added.

"Or the saltwater was used to frame Nathaniel," I said. "All of these are plausible."

"But why frame Nathaniel?" Alex asked.

"I'm not sure," I said honestly. "I don't know of anyone angry enough at Nathaniel to want him out of the picture." I drained the last of my coffee and pushed the mug away so I wouldn't be tempted to pour a third cup. "The other thing we need to talk about with Monte and Nathaniel are the hidden compartments and stolen items inside."

"Looks like you guys will be busy today," Alex said. "Grant and I have a lead on the theft on the east side of the island, so we'll probably be working that case. Just call if you need us."

Needles flew over to land on my shoulder. *"We got it all under control, Gargoyle."*

19

I texted Monte and told him I needed to see both him and Nathaniel when I arrived at the circus. He promised to have Nathaniel there, even if it meant pulling his personal performance and having Esta step in for him.

"What's this about?" Nathaniel demanded the minute Zoie, Needles, and I entered Monte's tent office. "I'm supposed to have a show in ten minutes."

"I'm afraid that might need to be put on hold," I said.

Monte placed a hand on Nathaniel's arm. "I told you, Esta can handle the performance alone."

Nathaniel pursed his lips but didn't say anything else.

"Let's get down to business," I said. "We found the hidden compartments in Sebastian's puppets."

The two men glanced at each other, then quickly looked away.

"You don't seem surprised," Zoie mused.

Monte cleared his throat and nodded solemnly. "I didn't know until last night when Nathaniel came to me and said he needed to tell me something that could put the circus in jeopardy."

"When did you first learn about the hidden compartments?" I asked Nathaniel.

"About a week before Monte moved me to the escape artist tent. I'd pushed back on Sebastian, dropping enough hints that I think he knew I found it. Next thing I knew, he's got me pinned between his creepy puppets, and I swear, I thought they were going to rip me apart. He said if I ever told, he'd make sure the puppets didn't leave any trace of me behind. I was immediately moved to a different area."

Monte nodded. "Yes. I didn't know what the circumstances were that led Sebastian to state either he would quit or I would move Nathaniel, but I figured it was a fight. I decided to move Nathaniel."

"And I thank you every day for it," Nathaniel said. "But when you guys discovered Sebastian was murdered, I thought maybe I should warn Monte of what I knew about the puppets. I asked him if he'd had a chance to look inside before the police took them away, and he said no. I then told him why that might not be a good thing."

"So that was what they were discussing last night when I was that odious owl."

"I swear, I had no idea," Monte said.

I pulled out my phone and showed them a picture of some of the items inside the compartments. "Does any of this look familiar to either of you?"

Both men shook their heads.

"Now what?" Monte asked.

"We're still investigating," I said.

Monte sighed. "I think it's time for some changes." He ran his weathered hands over his face and looked solemnly at

Nathaniel. "It's time the younger generation stood up and took over." He gestured to Nathaniel. "I have Nathaniel and Brylee doing acts." He smiled weakly. "I'm not a complete idiot. I know about Ariella. I've been turning a blind eye to the self-medicating until she was ready to talk, but I'm going to encourage her to take someone under her wing. I know of a half-pixie, half-fairy who would love to learn to do aerials. Ariella could teach her amazing things on the silks."

"And Esta," Nathaniel pointed out with a bit of a bite.

Monte smiled and nodded. "Yes, Esta. I'd already planned on moving her to her own tent, but I was waiting until we left here to tell her of the surprise."

"That's all I have for you, Nathaniel," I said. "I just wanted to know when you learned about the compartments."

Nathaniel nodded. "Okay. And I'm sorry, Monte, that I never said anything to you about them until just now. I just had no proof Sebastian was stealing. He could have claimed they were gifts from women or family heirlooms, so I just kept my mouth shut and went to a different tent."

After Nathaniel left, I turned back to Monte. "Tell me about Tika and Sebastian."

Monte closed his eyes and dropped down into a chair. "I'm just getting too old for this." He gestured for Zoie and me to have a seat as well. "I couldn't believe it when Tika told me she was pregnant and that when she told Sebastian, he said he wanted nothing to do with her or the baby."

"Why not fire him?" Zoie asked.

"Even though the circus had only been open a little over a year at that time, the supernaturals flocked to Sebastian. He was quite gifted. We were still a small circus. Counting Sebastian, I had Tika and an escape artist." He let out a small laugh. "Not exactly a lot of attractions for circus-goers. If Sebastian left, the circus would fold. Tika knew it. That would mean not only would I be out of a job, but it would leave Tika and the baby out in the cold as well."

"So you kept him on," I stated.

Monte nodded solemnly. "I did. All these years, I put up with his intimidation and threats of leaving. I did my best to placate him."

"And now that Tika is dying," I said, "Brylee will need to keep her circus job more than ever."

Monte waved his hand dismissively in the air. "I've been covering a lot of Tika's special ingredients the healing witches and fairies need, and I will continue to do that for Tika until it's no longer needed."

"Are you aware Brylee and Sebastian were fighting Wednesday night?" I asked.

"Brylee didn't kill Sebastian!" Monte exclaimed.

"You sound certain," Zoie said.

"Because maybe he *killed Sebastian,"* Needles mused.

"I need to see the will, Monte," I said.

Monte lifted a hand to his head and shook it. "I'm so sorry. With everything going on, I completely forgot." He strolled over to his desk but bypassed it to stand near the tent wall. Whispering under his breath, the camouflage bubble he'd used to hide the safe fell away.

"I don't like anyone knowing I have this," Monte said by way of explanation. He waved his hand in front of the safe, and I heard a click. Seconds later, he opened the safe and withdrew an envelope, then used his magic to camouflage the safe once again.

"This is Sebastian's will," he said, handing me the sealed envelope.

After examining the envelope with more scrutiny, I determined it had not been tampered with. Breaking the seal, I withdrew the paper inside and read aloud.

"This is my last will and testament. To Monte, I leave my puppets. You will know what to do with them. And because I know if I leave all of my worldly possessions to you, Monte, you will just give them to Brylee, I'll just save you that task. Brylee Flare, the daughter of Tika Flare, will inherit everything I have, which amounts to approximately a hundred thousand in cash in a lockbox disclosed herein. This is by no means an admission of me being her father. I am just leaving her my possessions."

"This guy was a piece of work," Needles muttered.

"That's everything," I said. "He's signed it, so everything looks official."

"Do you think Brylee knew?" Needles mused. *"This is a huge motive for her to kill Sebastian. She can now pay for the potions to keep her mom alive."*

"Will you tell Brylee, or should I?" Monte asked.

"Monte, you have to know this goes to motive, right?" I said.

Monte's cheeks turned pink. "Brylee did not kill Sebastian. She may have hated him, but she wouldn't have killed him."

"Not even to keep her mom alive?" Zoie whispered.

Monte looked away, but remained silent.

"We'll tell Brylee," I said. "Thank you for your time, Monte."

The older man sighed and sat down in his chair. "I'm just getting too old."

We stepped outside and headed toward Brylee's tent. Before we reached it, Nathaniel's tent flap opened and Esta walked out, looking stunning in a sequined swimsuit. She laughed and shook hands with the supernaturals leaving the tent, and I had no problem seeing her in a more responsible role.

As the last of the attendees exited, Brylee Flare called out to Esta and jogged over to Nathaniel's tent.

"I guess we can tell Brylee the good news," I said, motioning for Zoie to follow me as Needles landed on my shoulder.

But as we drew closer, I could see that Esta and Brylee were in a heated discussion. When Brylee moved to enter the tent, Esta shook her head and blocked her way. Brylee and Esta grappled for a few seconds before Brylee let go, pointed a finger in Esta's face, then stormed off in the opposite direction.

"What do you suppose that was about?" Zoie whispered.

Before I could place a guess, Nathaniel exited his tent and stared after Brylee.

"Well, that was ominous," I muttered. "Let's head off Brylee so we can talk with her."

As we followed after Brylee, I noticed an imposing young man watching her as she retreated, a look of unrequited love and longing on his face. He was a hulking troll who looked to be in his early twenties. I was about to dismiss him until I saw Grigor call out to the boy.

"That must be Manny, his son," I said. "Let's go see about Grigor's alibi real quick."

We hurried over to where the two men stood talking. When they saw us, they both went quiet.

"I just have one quick question," I said. "Are you Manny, Grigor's son?"

The boy nodded but didn't say anything.

"Can you tell me where you were yesterday morning around 9:00?" I asked. "This would have been about fifteen minutes before the mandatory meeting in The Big Top."

Manny frowned and looked at his dad. "I came to Dad's tent. He always lifts weights to loosen up his muscles. I got there around 9:00, we did a set, and then we went to the meeting. Why?"

"I was just curious. Thank you for your time."

Manny nodded, but I didn't miss the way his eyes followed Brylee as she hurried toward the infirmary. And then I remembered Grigor talking about his son trying to impress one of the performers, and I had to wonder if maybe Manny didn't have a soft spot for Brylee. And if he did, how far would the young giant go to prove his love for her?

Would he kill her father for her?

20

"Hey, Brylee," Zoie called out as we hurried to catch up to her. "Wait up!"

Brylee turned and scowled. "What do you want?"

"Are you okay?" Zoie asked. "We couldn't help but see the argument you just had with Esta. Is everything okay?"

"As if you care."

"Not really," Needles said dryly.

"Of course we care," Zoie said.

Tears sprang to Brylee's eyes, and she quickly blinked them back. "I just wanted to talk to Nathaniel. I'm so upset and confused, and that—" She paused. "I just needed him. I just wanted to talk with him."

"So why didn't he talk to you?" I asked.

Brylee looked away and folded her arms across her chest. "Nathaniel and I had a thing about six months ago. It didn't last too long." She snorted. "Mainly because I found out he was only seeing me to make Sebastian angry. It's like those two had to get the last word or the last dig. And I was the pawn in Nathaniel's latest game."

Needles sprang from my shoulder. *"You said earlier you were looking for someone angry enough at Nathaniel to frame him for Sebastian's murder, Princess."*

"That sounds horrible, Brylee," Zoie said.

"Horrible doesn't even come close to how it feels. What's worse is that I'm pathetic because I still care for him."

"That's not pathetic," Zoie said. "You had feelings for Nathaniel and cared about him. That's not pathetic."

"Thanks for that," Brylee said. "Listen, I need to get back to my mom. Monte's giving me the afternoon off so I can sit with her."

"Real quick," I said. "What's the story with Esta? Are she and Nathaniel seeing each other?"

Brylee shrugged. "I don't know. Rumor is they are, but I've never seen anything that says Nathaniel is into her. Of course, Nathaniel is a lot like Sebastian…out for himself."

"One last thing," I said. "Did you know Sebastian was blackmailing your best friend, Ariella, regarding her condition?"

Brylee nodded. "Yes. I told her not to trust him when he came sniffing around."

I frowned. "What do you mean?"

"Sebastian liked to have dirt on everyone. He was the ultimate puppet master—or at least, that's what he liked to brag about. But the thing was, he had nothing on Ariella, so he had to take a different approach. He romanced her. Then, when he discovered her weakness, he used it to hurt her. He was a horrible person, and I'm embarrassed he was my father."

"Speaking of, Princess, are you going to tell her?"

"I just read Sebastian's last will and testament, Brylee," I said. "You might want to go see Monte, but I told him I would tell you."

"Tell me what?" she asked.

"You are pretty much Sebastian's sole heir. From what I understand, it's quite an extensive amount of money he's left you."

"Enough you should be able to help your mom," Zoie said softly.

Brylee covered her mouth with her hands, her eyes huge. "Are you serious? Sebastian left me enough money to help keep my mom alive?"

I nodded. "He did. Monte knows all about it."

With a joyful scream, Brylee threw her arms around Zoie, then took off running toward Monte's office tent.

"What do you think?" Needles asked. *"Do you think she knew she might be in Sebastian's will, so she decided to roll the dice and kill her own father and take that chance?"*

"Not sure yet," I said honestly.

"Since we worked through lunch, how about you get me a snack, Princess?" Needles said.

I rolled my eyes. "You're hungry again?"

"I'm always up for an extra salty pretzel."

* * *

"Now who do you want to talk with?" Zoie asked once our snacks had been consumed.

"Let's go talk with Manny," I said, tossing my wrapper into the trash receptacle. "I want to know just how much he likes Brylee and how far he'd go for her."

We took off toward the kiddie area of the circus. I knew he

worked the teacups, and they weren't hard to miss, seeing as how they were three feet in the air.

We were almost to the teacups when Mr. and Mrs. Mystic darted out in front of us, each hollering after their five kids.

"Oh, Shayla," Mrs. Mystic said in a harried voice, patting her frayed hair into place. "My husband and I thought the circus would be a good idea, but I'm afraid this might be the death of us."

"Have kids, they said," Mr. Mystic snickered. "It'll be fun, they said."

Zoie, Needles, and I laughed as we waved goodbye to their retreating forms. We headed over to where Manny stood next to a twenty-something witch. She was using magic to make the teacups go up and down and twirl around in a slow motion, causing the four teacups to spin gracefully.

"Hey, Manny," I said. "Remember me?"

Manny looked warily at me and nodded. "Of course."

"I wanted to ask you some questions about Brylee Flare," I said.

"I'll give you guys some privacy," the younger witch said before distancing herself a good six feet away.

"What about Brylee?" Manny asked.

"Do you know her well?" I asked.

Manny shrugged and shook his head. "No, not really."

"You knew Sebastian Blackwood was her father?" Zoie asked.

"Yeah."

"He's not a talkative troll, is he?" Needles mused.

"Do you like Brylee?" I asked.

Manny's neck and cheeks took on a reddish hue. "Of course I like her. She's nice."

"No, Manny," I said, my patience wearing thin. "Do you *like* her?"

Manny kicked at the ground with his massive shoe. "I suppose I do. Why?"

"Would you do anything for her?" I asked.

Manny frowned and scratched his head. "Like what?"

"And he's not the sharpest tool in the shed," Needles said.

"Like, if she asked you to kill Sebastian, would you?" I asked.

Manny's mouth dropped, and his eyes went wide. "Are you crazy? I mean, I like her, but I wouldn't kill for her. Why would you even ask me something like that?"

"It's just a question we had to ask," Zoie said.

"Yeah? Well, I didn't like it. It's a terrible thought even to say out loud."

"You're right," I said. "That's all the questions we have."

"Yeah, I don't think he's our guy," Needles said from my shoulder.

I heard my name being called, and I turned around to see Tommy Trollman hurrying my way, Mia riding on his shoulders. Next to him was Jacob, Pepper's ten-year-old son.

"Look at you, Tommy," I said. "Playing hooky on a Saturday afternoon?"

Tommy laughed, causing Mia to squeal even louder. "I suggested to Pepper and the kids we have some fun today."

I glanced over at Jacob. "And are you having fun?"

The boy nodded and smiled. "I am. This is my first time at a supernatural circus."

"Hey, Pepper," I said casually.

The pretty woman smiled and tucked a loose strand of hair behind her ear. "Hey, Shayla."

Tommy had been dating Pepper for almost four months now. She'd fled with her two kids to hide out on Enchanted Island when her abusive ex-husband had become even more violent. She said he'd always taken his anger out on her when their son was born a Normal despite having supernatural parents. But when their daughter came along, showing exceptional magical powers by the age of one, her husband lashed out even more and would also take his anger out on Jacob. She'd had enough and fled the supernatural town she lived in, hiding out on Enchanted Island. She now managed a knickknack store that Tommy owned. And as far as I knew…her ex-husband had no idea where she or the children were.

"What's been your favorite thing so far?" I asked Jacob.

He grinned. "Definitely the unicorns and the phoenix. We just came from The Big Top. It was really neat."

"Unicorns!" Mia echoed.

"Where are you guys headed now?" Zoie asked.

"Teacups!" Mia exclaimed.

Jacob rolled his eyes. "Baby rides."

Tommy put his massive hand on the boy's head and ruffled his hair. "I'll take you on a couple of the adult rides soon enough. I promise."

"I'd love to see Tommy on the adult teacups," Needles snickered.

We waved goodbye and headed toward The Big Top. Now that Manny wasn't high on my list of suspects, we needed to regroup. We were almost at The Big Top when Madame Seraphina stepped out from her tent and pointed a gnarled finger at me.

"Heed my warning, Witch! Stay away from the porcupine. He will kill you!"

"That's it!" Needles snarled as he leaped from my shoulder,

his wings glowing red and black. *"I'm going to take out an eye and carve out her lying tongue."*

"You'll do no such thing, Needles," I said as the seer hurried away.

"Give me one good reason why not, Princess?" Needles demanded.

"Because I vote we have an early dinner," I said.

"Food? Why didn't you say so earlier?" Needles dropped his two quills and hurried back over to my shoulder. *"I could eat a little something."*

Zoie laughed. "Can't you always?"

21

"I can't believe I'm going to say this," Zoie said, patting her stomach. "But I'm almost tired of circus food. If I eat one more funnel cake, I might explode."

"*Well, explode in the opposite direction,*" Needles said. "*I'm finishing my supper.*"

I laughed. "I understand what you're saying. Last night, I was eager for your dad's honey-glazed chicken salad."

"Look, Shayla!" Zoie exclaimed. "Isn't that Brylee running toward the infirmary tent?"

I followed her finger and nodded. "Yes, and that's a full-out sprint."

"Do you think...do you think it's her mom?" Zoie whispered, fear and sadness laced in her voice. "Do you think Tika died?"

"I hope not," I said. "Now that Brylee can actually afford treatments, that would be an awful blow."

We finished our dinner and made small talk with some of the citizens before strolling over to Brylee's pyrotechnic tent. My eyes widened when I saw Esta Topaz greeting people and motioning them inside.

"What's going on?" I asked.

Esta shrugged. "Monte said there was an emergency, and Brylee needed to go. He asked me to come down here and fill in for her." She gestured inside the tent. "I don't know how to do fire stuff, so I'm just going to do small things. I can use my magic to perform some tricks. I just hope I'm not awful."

Zoie reached over and patted Esta's arm. "I'm sure you'll be just fine."

"Okay, well, let's hope so," Esta said with a wave as she turned and went inside the tent.

"Let's go see if Ariella knows what's going on," I said.

The sign on Ariella's tent said her next performance was in thirty minutes, so I opened the flap and motioned Zoie to go ahead of me. I blinked in surprise at the sight of Ariella crying and crawling around on her hands and knees.

"Everything okay?" I asked.

Ariella looked up and shook her head. "I've lost one of my moon earrings Sebastian gave me. I always leave them in the same spot right before I perform." She blew out a breath and gave a shaky laugh as she staggered to her feet. "Okay, maybe it's not just about the earring. Brylee's mom went into cardiac arrest." She swiped at the tears on her cheeks. "I'm just emotional, and I'm still waiting to hear the news about Tika."

I gave her a small smile. "I'm sorry about both the earring and Tika. We'll hope for the best."

"Thank you," Ariella said. "I'll let Brylee know you wish her mom well."

The next few hours dragged on, and just as the park was getting ready to close, Zoie, Needles, and I made our way to the infirmary tent. Like Zoie, I really didn't want to hear the outcome, but it was inevitable.

At the entrance, I saw Monte and Brylee embracing. I could see he was whispering words to her as he patted her back while she sobbed on his shoulder.

"I heard what happened," I said. "I'm sorry."

Brylee took a step back from Monte's arms and wiped her eyes and cheeks. "Thank you. I wasn't expecting good news when I got here, and it wasn't. But the pixies have been working double time, and there are healing witches who haven't left Mom's side. They were able to stabilize her, but she's critical."

Monte laid a hand on Brylee's shoulder. "I was just telling Brylee I will sell one or two of Sebastian's puppets to get us some cash quickly so we can get our hands on the pricier ingredients."

"That's very kind of you, Monte," I said.

Zoie nodded. "It really is. It's too bad the puppets have to go, but Tika will appreciate it."

"Tika is worth it," Monte said. "Which is why I've told Brylee to take a small leave of absence. Even if it's just for a couple of weeks, we'll be able to get someone to fill in for her."

Fresh tears filled Brylee's eyes. "I hate leaving you in the lurch like this, Monte, but I really appreciate it. I know tomorrow is our last day here on Enchanted Island, so it'll only be a couple performances that need covered."

"Can we see your mom?" I asked.

Brylee nodded. "Sure. I just came out to get some fresh air and talk with Monte. I'll be in shortly."

"Why are we going in to see Tika?" Needles asked from my shoulder.

"Because it's the nice thing to do," I whispered.

We quietly made our way to the back of the tent where Tika's closed-off curtained room was. Pulling the drape aside, the three of us entered the somber room.

Vaida looked up and shook her head, her brows furrowed in concern. "We've just gotten her stable. I don't think she's up to talking."

"We don't need to ask her any questions." I scrutinized Vaida's anxious face and frowned. Circus people were a private bunch, but I was beginning to understand you had to read between the lines sometimes. "Do I *need* to speak to Tika?"

Vaida wrung her hands, her wings glowing yellow and blue as they fluttered frantically. "No, Miss. No reason at all."

"Is she acting strange?" Needles mused. *"Because I get the feeling she's acting strange. And is it me, or does it smell off in here?"*

I casually strolled over to Tika's bedside and admired the flowers. "Are these from Brylee? Or did Tika have visitors today?"

"She had a couple visitors," Vaida said.

"What aren't you saying, Vaida? I get the feeling—" I broke off when I saw something glittering on the floor near the table where the flowers were sitting. Bending down, I picked up the object and frowned.

It was a moon earring.

Had Ariella been here to visit Tika?

"Talk to me, Vaida," I demanded, half-pleading.

"I know Tika is dying," the pixie said, wringing her hands. "But with her type of condition, cardiac arrest is not normal. I just don't understand why that happened."

I leaned in to smell the wildflowers and reeled backward.

"Princess!" Needles demanded. *"What's wrong?"*

I blinked back tears and swallowed, closing my eyes against the wave of nausea and dizziness.

"What's happening?" Vaida asked.

I let out a small moan. "There are Tears of the Siren in the water inside the vase."

"Tears of the Siren?" Zoie asked. "Is it poisonous?"

I nodded. "Yes. One drop in water produces an invisible gas-like release."

"I knew there was a weird smell in here!"

"That's not possible," Vaida said, her wings buzzing so frantically, I was afraid she'd shoot to the top of the tent.

"Why couldn't Vaida smell it?" Zoie asked. "Or me, for that matter?"

"It's a silent killer," I said. "I am more vulnerable to plant poisons because of my connection with Black Forest King. Most humans and supernaturals have no idea they are even smelling it until it's too late."

"Is it easy to get?" Zoie asked.

"It grows wild, so yes."

"That could explain why Tika went into cardiac arrest," Vaida said frantically. "Oh, what do I do? What do I do?"

"I'll handle it," I said. "But I've got to know, Vaida. Who visited Tika today?" I opened my hand to show Needles and Zoie what I'd picked up off the floor. "Recognize this?"

Zoie's eyes went wide. "Do you suppose that's the moon earring Ariella was looking for?"

I nodded, then turned to Vaida to repeat my question. "Who all visited Tika, Vaida?"

"There were a few visitors," Vaida admitted.

22

"So who is it?" Zoie asked as we hurried out of the infirmary tent. "Ariella? You found her earring on the ground. Is she the killer?"

"I'm not exactly sure," I said. "I know Monte isn't our killer. No way would he attempt to kill Tika. I think we can eliminate Grigor as well. This attempt on Tika's life doesn't fit with why he might kill Sebastian. He was never angry at Tika or Brylee. In fact, his son likes Brylee."

"So that leaves Ariella, Nathaniel, and Esta," Zoie said. "All three visited Tika today, according to Vaida."

"I'll find Ariella. You and Needles track down Nathaniel and Esta. With the circus now closed, they might still be in their performance tent. Round them up and let's light a fire under them."

"Going with roasting alive," Needles said as he leaped off my shoulder, his wings glowing red. *"Good choice, Princess."*

I snorted. "Just go get those two. I'll round up Ariella. Let's all meet back at Monte's office."

"Be careful, Princess," Needles said. *"It looks like Ariella might be our killer."*

"Same to you two," I said. "Keep your eyes open."

We split up and headed for our respective tents. As I neared Ariella's shelter, I slowed down and tried to put the clues together. I'd always felt most of them had been planted…but why? Our first clue in Sebastian's tent had been the standing saltwater. Makes sense if the killer wanted us to look at Esta or Nathaniel. But the attempt on Tika's life and moon earring was different. Was the killer trying to set up Ariella with the dropped earring? Did they want her gone? And who would benefit with Tika out of the way? And why kill her now? Until a few hours ago, it was thought she wouldn't live much longer, but was the killer afraid Tika might continue to live if Brylee could now afford the medication? So was the killer trying to harm Brylee by killing her mom?

If I went with Ariella being the killer and her motive being Sebastian threatening to spill her secret before she was ready to tell *and* the fact he broke up with her…then it made sense why she might plant saltwater in Sebastian's tent to throw us off. But what was the motive to kill Tika? She and Brylee were best friends. Why kill the best friend's mom?

I pushed open Ariella's tent and stepped inside. It was completely empty except for the two people standing near a row of silks. Well, one was standing…the other was bleeding from the head and looked disoriented as she swayed on her feet.

"I'll make it quick…I promise," Esta said. "I've already left one of your earrings I lifted earlier today in Tika's room just in case she *does* pull through, and with this note you're leaving behind, it should clear everything else up. How you were so overcome with jealousy—Sebastian never committing to you because deep down you suspected he always had a thing for Tika

—and then when you learned he left everything in his will to Brylee and not you, you just couldn't take the betrayal anymore."

"That's pretty weak," I said, stepping farther into the room. "You must think I'm an idiot if I'd believe that story."

"You're gonna want to step back," Esta said, pulling Ariella close to her. "I won't hesitate to kill her."

"Why? Why kill Sebastian and try to kill Tika and Ariella? None of this makes sense."

"Why?" Esta screamed, sparks shooting out of her fingertips. "I'll tell you *why*. Because it's *my* time now! I'm tired of being the assistant. It should be *my* time." She slapped one hand against her chest as she struggled to keep Ariella upright. "By killing off Sebastian, a spot opens up. I thought the saltwater would point you to Nathaniel, but when it became apparent you weren't going to arrest him so I could have his place, I decided to open up another spot. By killing Tika, Brylee would be too distraught to work, so I could take over her tent, and by setting up Ariella with the earring, I figured you'd maybe think she planted the saltwater, and then her spot would be open. I should have *plenty* of choices." She narrowed her eyes at me. "But now I'm going to have to kill you and make it look like you and Ariella fought. So much for the note I took pains in writing! Way to mess everything up, you stupid witch!"

Where was Needles when I needed him? Normally, he'd be yammering away in my ear about how crazy she was, and that would give me the motivation I'd need to take Esta out. "How did you manage to kill Sebastian in the timeframe you had? Did you really go get the garment in your tent?"

Esta shook her head and laughed. "You still haven't figured it all out, have you? *I* was the one who planted Grigor's Warhammer in Sebastian's tent. I'd been running errands for Nathaniel, like I was *his* to boss around. I'd had enough! So I put my plan into motion. What I hadn't planned on was PADA detectives working the circus!"

"And what was your plan?" I asked, glossing over the PADA reference.

Esta huffed and rolled her eyes. "Steal the Warhammer, drop the strings as a clue, kill Sebastian, and start making some serious changes around here. I loosened the straps on the garment ahead of time and when I told Nathaniel I'd take them to my tent to tighten, I didn't really leave it in my tent the next morning. I took it with me, hid it behind our tent, and then I had plenty of time to sneak into Sebastian's tent. I didn't know if I'd kill him that day or wait for a better time, but when I got to Sebastian's tent, he was meditating. His eyes were closed, he was already sitting down…it was perfect! So I used my magic and enchanted some strings near him, and the rest is history. I waited until I knew I'd be cutting it close to the meeting for a more solid alibi, and then I picked up the garment and ran to The Big Top."

I shook my head and took another step closer to the two women…until I was just a few feet away. "This was all so pointless. Did you know after the circus closes tomorrow night, Monte was going to announce it was time for the younger generation—that's you—to step up and take over? You were going to get your own tent."

"*Liar!*" Esta screamed.

"I'm not—"

My words cut off when I felt a silk wrap around my neck and squeeze…hard. For a second, I was too stunned and panicked to do anything more than claw at the silk, trying to loosen it. Esta tossed Ariella onto the ground and used her magic to compel the other silks to start wrapping around my body…squeezing me like a snake does his prey. I closed my eyes and tried to use my own magic to rip the silks, but I was quickly losing consciousness.

"Unhand my princess!"

I heard Needles, but I couldn't see him. The silks were literally wrapped around my head and covering my eyes. But, again, the fact I couldn't breathe was a more pressing matter, I felt. Hysteria bubbled up inside me, and I laughed at the direction of my thoughts. To be taken out by an enchanted silk was *not* how I wanted to go out.

"Go away!" I heard Esta scream. "Get away from her!"

"*After I cut you free, Princess,*" Needles panted in my head, "*I'm going to cut her into a million pieces!*"

I wanted to encourage him...but I could barely keep a thought in my head. If I had been able to see, I was sure I'd be seeing black spots in my vision.

I was suddenly aware of air rushing into my lungs, and I opened my mouth to suck in even more. I could smell copper, and a few seconds later, when the last of the silks had been cut from my head, I could see blood dripping down my body.

"*Sorry, Princess. I was using my quills to cut the silks as fast as I could, and I'm afraid I cut you a couple times on your face and neck.*"

"It's okay," I whispered, looking down and frowning. "How did I get up here?"

"I think you levitated yourself in your panic," Zoie said. "I've got Ariella. I'm sorry, Shayla. But I felt I needed to stay and make sure Ariella and you would be okay. But Esta can't get far. Are you able to chase her down?"

"*I'm going to chase her down and filet her!*" Needles exclaimed, his wings glowing a deep crimson.

I wiped the blood from my face and neck and slowly lowered myself to the ground. "I've got this." When my feet touched the ground, I closed my eyes and called out to Blaze, hoping I could make a connection with the fiery phoenix.

"Blaze. This is Princess Shayla Loci-Stone. Can you hear me?"

"I hear you. What can I do for you, Princess?"

"I need you to get in the air. Find Esta and tell me where she's heading. Please, hurry!"

"I'm on it, Princess."

I turned to Zoie. "I got Blaze in the air. Needles and I can handle Esta if you want to call your dad for me."

"I just did," Zoie said. "But *you* might want to hurry before he comes flying in here and stealing your fun."

"Let's go, Princess! Time to kick some mer-witch butt!"

Needles settled on my shoulder as I sprinted out of Ariella's tent and into the night. There were still a few employees hanging around, clustered in groups, not paying us any attention.

I heard a call in the air and looked up. Blaze was circling to the right of Ariella's tent, heading toward the encampment.

"Do you want me to stop her?" Blaze asked.

"Just don't kill her," I said.

From overhead, a massive stream of fire shot toward the ground, causing a few supernaturals to scream and take cover. I kept running, closing the gap on Esta. When she whirled around to face me, I was ready for her. I lifted my hands and sent a stream of magic her way…knocking her off her feet.

"That's for nearly suffocating me," I growled as I unhooked my Binder from around my waist and tossed it over her.

"Did I miss all the—what happened to your face?" Alex demanded as he landed next to me and shifted back to his human form. "Are you hurt?"

"I'm fine," I said. "Got our killer as well."

A high-pitched laughter sounded behind me. "I told you to stay away from that porcupine." Madame Seraphina cackled again and shook her head. "He'd end up attacking you and making you bleed, I said."

Needles whipped out two quills from his back, his wings glowing red and black. *"That's it, Princess. I'm going to—"*

I started to laugh. "It's okay, Needles. I'm sure when she saw it in her vision, it *did* look like you were attacking me."

Needles' wings drooped, and he fluttered down to my shoulder. *"I'm sorry, Princess."*

I heard Alex on his phone, calling PADA for an escort. "It's fine, Needles. I'm just glad you were able to get to me. I hadn't been that scared in a long time. Suffocating isn't pleasant."

"What's this?" Alex demanded. "Who suffocated you?"

I laughed. "All in good time. Let's go get Zoie and get Ariella some help…then find Monte and tell him the bad news."

23

"Thanks for the healing touch." I threw my arms around Mom and hugged her before turning and hugging Dad's trunk. "I could have done it myself, but I knew you two would want to be involved."

"*I hate you needed us,*" Dad said. "*But you're right.*"

"*Again, Princess, I'm so sorry,*" Needles said as he fluttered down Dad's branches and landed on my shoulder.

I ran my hand down Needles' face. "I can't tell you how thankful I am you came in when you did, Needles."

"*As am I, old friend,*" Dad murmured.

"Me too," Mom said.

"Even I think you deserve an extra bag of pretzels," Alex joked as he leaned over and kissed my temple.

It had been three days since the circus closed, and one day since they'd packed up and left Enchanted Island. While Monte was heartbroken about Esta being the killer, he was encouraged by the fact Tika was out of critical care.

When GiGi and a couple other witches heard about the expensive, rare ingredients Tika needed, they banded together and made a couple potions for her until new ingredients could be ordered for her.

Ariella was healing nicely and told me she was excited to work with the half fairy, half pixie Monte had hooked her up with. It was time to pass on the torch, she'd said.

"The best news was with the money Sebastian left Brylee, her mom should be able to get prolonged care," I said. "Which will add years to her life."

"That is good news," Dad said.

"I also had a chance to talk with Brylee privately," I said. "I reminded her that just because Nathaniel treated her unkindly, didn't mean every guy was like that."

"You played matchmaker, Princess?" Needles mused.

I shrugged. "A little. She knew I was talking about Manny, and she said when things calmed down with her mom, she'd give it more thought."

"Can't do more than that," Needles said.

"Did Shayla tell you about the young man Harlow is dating?" Mom asked Dad.

Dad chuckled. *"I heard he is the exact opposite of young Harlow. I cannot wait to meet him."*

"He's colorful," Needles said. *"Like me. I liked him."*

"There's a lot coming up," Mom said. "We have the twins' first birthday party, GiGi's bridal shower, you and Alex will be celebrating your one-year anniversary, and GiGi is already on me about a bachelorette party."

Needles did a somersault in the air. *"Bachelorette party! All right! I'm going to GiGi's bachelorette party. No way I'm missing this one. I always get stuck with the guys, and they're boring! I don't care if I have to hide away like I did when I went on your honeymoon, Princess. I'm going to GiGi's bachelorette party."*

"Fine by me," Alex said with a grin.

I narrowed my eyes at Alex. "He's not going."

"Wanna bet!"

Before I could argue, Needles zipped up into Dad's branches. Dad and Mom both laughed.

"This Dominic is helping to plan the twins' birthday party?" Dad mused.

"Yes," I said. "He seems very excited."

"Do you know where it will be held?" Dad asked.

"No idea," I admitted. "Do you know, Mom?"

Mom shook her head. "I don't think Serena has gotten that far in her planning."

"You could always have it here, in Black Forest."

I blinked in surprise. "Really, Dad? You wouldn't mind? It may mean Harlow's new boyfriend will need to be here as well."

"Why do you think I offered?" Dad said. *"I would like to meet this fellow who dresses like a rainbow and who puts a small smile on our young Harlow's face."*

I grinned. "I'm sure Serena would love to have the party out here."

Dozens of fireflies swarmed over my head, causing Alex to laugh.

"A birthday party?"

"Will there be cake?"

"And cotton candy?"

"Can we help with the party?"

"Thanks, Dad." I turned and wrapped my arms around his trunk, resting my head against the rough bark. "For everything."

One of Dad's massive branches lowered and carefully

stroked my back. *"You are welcome, Daughter of my Heart. Now, about GiGi's bachelorette party."*

* * *

Are you ready for the next book in the series? Then click here and get *Deadly Flame* and find out what happens when Harlow's new boyfriend finds himself embroiled in a murder mystery! The were-witch twins are *not* going to be happy if their first birthday party is put on hold! Deadly Flame

* * *

MORE PADA-World paranormal cozy series by Jenna St. James

SPINOFF!! Love the idea of a Valkyrie witch teaming up with a Fallen Angel to solve crimes? Then the paranormal cozy series, A Kara Hilder Mystery, should be right up your alley! A spinoff from the A Witch in the Woods, this crime-solving duo not only works for their supernatural town of Mystic Cove, but they also work for the Paranormal Apprehension and Detention Agency—which means they travel undercover to take down bad guys. Click here to read Book 1, *Sounds of Murder*: Sounds of Murder

. . .

SPINOFF! What happens when a mermaid-witch detective teams up with a treasure-hunting demigod with a snarky miniature glow-in-the-dark dragon named Glo? Find out in this humorous paranormal cozy series that is yet another spinoff from the A Witch in the Woods in the PADA world. Click here and get book 1, *Tangled Waters,* from the Enchanted Waters Mystery series: Tangled Waters

When you join Jenna's newsletter, you'll receive a FREE box set of Grant & Serena's trilogy. http://www.jennastjames.com/.

Facebook Author Page for Jenna St. James: facebook.com/jennastjamesauthor

Made in United States
Cleveland, OH
02 May 2025